The Dear Departed

Selected Short Stories

Brian Moore

turnpike
books

'A Vocation' first published in *Tamarack Review* (Autumn 1956),
'Grieve for the Dear Departed' first published in *The Atlantic*
(August 1959), 'Uncle T' first published in *Gentleman's Quarterly*
(November 1960), 'Lion of the Afternoon' first published in *The
Atlantic* (November 1957), 'Fly Away Finger, Fly Away Thumb' first
published in *London Mystery Magazine* (September 1953), 'Off the
Track' first published in *Ten for Wednesday Night* (ed. Robert Weaver,
McClelland and Stewart Ltd, 1961), 'Hearts and Flowers' first
published in *The Spectator* (November 24th 1961), 'Preliminary Pages
for a Work of Revenge' first published in *Midstream* (Winter 1961)

First published in Great Britain in 2020 by Turnpike Books

turnpikebooks@gmail.com

ISBN 9781916254701

Typeset in Plantin by MRules

Printed and bound by
Clays Ltd, Elcograf S.p.A.

Brian Moore was born in Belfast on August 25th 1921. In 1940 he volunteered for Belfast's Air Raid Precautions Unit and went on to join the British Ministry of War Transport in 1943 and served in France, Italy, north Africa. Near the end of the Second World War Moore visited Auschwitz as it was liberated and remained in Poland after the War with the United Nations Relief and Rehabilitation Administration.

Moore emigrated to Canada in 1948, and adopted Canadian citizenship in 1953, where he became a journalist and worked for the *Montreal Gazette* from 1949 to 1955.

The Lonely Passion of Judith Hearne was published in 1955 and was awarded the Authors' Club First Novel Award. He moved to the USA in 1959, first settling in New York before moving to California in 1965 where he worked as a screenwriter on Alfred Hitchcock's *Torn Curtain*.

He was shortlisted for the Booker Prize three times, for *The Doctor's Wife*, *The Colour of Blood* and *Lies of Silence* and was awarded the James Tait Black Memorial Prize in 1975 for *The Great Victorian Collection* and the Sunday Express Book of the Year in 1987 for *The Colour of Blood*.

Brian Moore died in 1999.

CONTENTS

A VOCATION

In the beginning was the Word. And the Word was 'No.'
All things came from that beginning. 'No, don't do that,
Joe,' Mama said. 'No, not now, Joe,' Daddy said.

Then there was God. Who is God? The catechism
said: *God is the Creator and Sovereign Lord of heaven and
earth and of all things.* You must learn your catechism by
heart. The big words will be explained later, when you go
to school. *God is everywhere and He judges our most secret
thoughts and actions*, the catechism said. God will reward
the good and punish the wicked. God doesn't like little
boys who hit their sisters. God is good. God save us.
God bless us. Merciful God, will you come away from
that stove, Joe. No, you can't go out today. No, God bless
us, what's the matter with you now? No, you can't have
another apple. Oh, for God's sake, let the child alone.

There was This World. The first question in the catechism was:

Q: Who made the world?
A: God.

The world was sweetie shops, Alexandra Park, the Antrim Road, Royal Avenue, Newington School, Miss Casey's garden, and the big pond in the waterworks. All these things were part of Belfast and Belfast was in Ireland. Dublin was in Ireland too. It was a whole day in the car to go to Dublin and come back.

Then there was the Next World. It was the only one that counted, Mama said. The next world was heaven and hell. And purgatory.

Q: What is purgatory?
A: A place or state of punishment in the other life, where some souls suffer for a time before they can go to heaven.

And there was limbo for the babies who were not baptized. Mama sometimes declared to heaven. She declared that you would try the patience of a saint, let alone hers. In the next world there was God the Father, and God the Son, and God the Holy Ghost, who was a bird. But the catechism said *They are only one God, having but one and the same divine nature.* Father Owens said it would be easier if you did not try to understand it now, I repeat, it will be easier later. Learn it now and the sense will come. Know it by heart. Stop talking. In the Next World there was Our Lady, Saint Patrick, Saint Joseph, and there was the Divine Infant Jesus. You made him sad when you were bad. Good boys who said their prayers and did not try the patience of a saint would go to heaven. To the Next World. It was the only one that counted.

There was sin. It was an awful thing in the sight of God.

Lies were sins. Losing your temper was a sin. Calling Mary a Dirty Pig was a sin. It was a sin to tell a lie. There was a song about that. It was a sin to steal Rory O'Hare's bike. That was a sin you got beaten for. It was a sin if you did not go to Mass on Sundays and Holy Days. But everybody went. Still, it was a Mortal Sin if you did not go. A Mortal Sin made the soul black and rotten in the sight of God. If you did not wipe that sin off by a good confession, you would be condemned to Everlasting Hell with the Devil and all his Fallen Angels.

There was impurity. That was the worst sin. That was what *you* did. Impurity. Sins like murder and idolatry were only in books. The catechism said that Impurity was *all immodest looks, words or actions and everything that is contrary to chastity.* It said *all immodest songs, discourses, novels, comedies, and plays* were forbidden by the Sixth Commandment. *It is sinful to join in them, to encourage them or to be present at them,* the catechism said. They were immediate occasions, Father Owens said. And he said other immediate occasions were *lascivious looks and touches, idleness, bad company, and whatever tends to inflame the passions.* Learn it off by heart, he said. You could look up the words in the front of the Lesson, if you did not understand them, Father Owens said. All the fellows looked them up. *Lascivious*: immodest, *passions*: bad inclinations, *amusements*: plays. Well, anyway, Father Owens said, Impurity is the sin against the Holy Ghost. It blackened the soul. If Father Owens knew how impure those thoughts were, he would faint, so he would. It was the only sin the priests asked about in confession. How many times? You must promise me never to do that again, will you promise me that? You will put these thoughts away, my child, won't you? Yes, Father. I will not sin. I am heartily sorry. I will not do it. No. That was impurity.

There was your Immortal Soul. If you committed that sin again, you endangered your Immortal Soul. That is the only thing that counts. What doth it profit a man if he gain the whole world and suffer the loss of his soul?

Remember, Joe, it's the next world that counts. You may think you're a big fellow in this world, but if you haven't made your peace with God, what does it matter?

There was Eternity. It was, the missioner said, something that the mind boggled at. It was the flames of hell for a time that was not time. Forever. Our feeble intellects could not even begin to grasp how long that was. Consider that word: eternity. Keep it always before you. What, I repeat, what mean the follies, the pomps, the tiny triumphs of this world of ours, what do they mean in the light of eternity, of eternal damnation?

Q: Is it sinful to have unchaste thoughts when there is no intention or desire to indulge them by any criminal actions?

A: They are always very dangerous and when entertained deliberately and with pleasure may defile the soul like criminal actions.

Now, since you have come to seek my advice in this matter, I am going to ask you one question, Joe, you said your name was Joe, did you not? Very well. In school you probably learned your Christian's Daily Exercise by heart, did you not? Now, here is a question from those exercises: *How should you finish the day?*

I should observe great modesty in going to bed: entertain myself with the thoughts of death; and endeavour to compose myself to rest at the foot of the cross and to give my last thoughts to my crucified Saviour.

I see you have not forgotten your exercise. Very good. Now, tell me truthfully, did you think of those precepts the last time you went to bed?

No, you did not. Now, promise me you will remember them in your future. Promise me too, that you will pray to Our Lady for guidance when such thoughts come into your mind. You will not indulge in those thoughts again, I am sure. Go now, and remember to say a little prayer for me.

There was Holy Communion. Tomorrow, when the retreat was over, they would all receive the Body and Blood of Our Blessed Lord. The rule of silence was ended. Every boy in school was in the State of Grace. Keep those precepts in mind, the missioner said. Remember your last end. You may die tonight and face that end. You must always remain in the state of grace. What doth it profit a man if he gain the whole world and suffer the loss of his soul?

The next world is the only one that counts, Joe.

They were sitting on the edge of the cinder track on the far side of the Big Field. The retreat was over, the rule of silence had been removed. Danny Boyle spat on his bare knee. He took out a dirty handkerchief and rubbed the spittle in, to take the black dirt off. He pulled up his socks and stuck the hanky in his pants pocket.

'He put the wind up me. But you know, there's something in what he says, though. About the next world and this one.'

Joe pulled a blade of grass off the bank and stuck it between his front teeth. 'I know.'

'All codding aside, Joe, it's the only thing that counts.'

'I know.'

'Sure, the best thing would be to die young. Say, as young as seven. Then you'd be in the state of grace. But still, seven is the age of reason. Six would be better.'

'I'm twelve,' Joe said.

'Sure, that's not old. Just think, the Seniors have more sins than the likes of us.'

'Even us,' Joe said. 'We'd have to go to purgatory.'

'Aye, but we're young, that wouldn't be such a long penance for you and me. If you live to be old, you can't help committing a lot more sins.'

'Even so. Even for us, purgatory would be long enough.'

'Well then, the best thing to do would be to join an order – as soon as you had your school leaving cert. If a fellow joined an order he'd be praying morning, noon, and night. He'd have all his life to pile up indulgences against the time he'd have to spend in purgatory. So, when you die an old man you'd probably have hardly any time in purgatory at all. You'd go straight to heaven.'

'You might.'

'If a fellow was wise, that's what he'd do. After all, it's the next world that counts.'

'That would be the best thing,' Joe said. 'To be a priest. An order priest. It would be safest.'

GRIEVE FOR THE
DEAR DEPARTED

Telegrams had been coming all day, punctuation marks of
sympathy in the long story of people who nosed into the
house from every part of Dublin, piled up wet overcoats
in the hall, exchanged handshakes and gazed with doggy
sincerity at the dead man's family in the parlour, tiptoed
into the spare room to mumble prayers and praise, then
back to the hall to meet new people as they were leaving.
There had never been so many visitors on any day of
Daniel Kelleher's life.

So, the cable from New York was not noticed until
evening. Then, when her mother had gone to lie down,
Peggy took several envelopes into the kitchen. When she
opened the fifth and saw whom it was from, she hurried
upstairs to the big bedroom, its door ajar, no light inside.

'Are you asleep, Mama?'

'No, no.'

She went in. The blinds had not been drawn, and in the

failed light between day and dusk she saw her mother's outline by the window, sitting in the old wicker-and-stuffing chair in which she had nursed every one of them.

'What is it? Is that you, Peggy?'

'Mama, there's a cable from Michael. Will I put on the light?'

'Just the bed lamp. And hand me my glasses.'

Mrs Kelleher took the cable from her daughter, held it at arm's length, her lips moving as she puzzled at the strips of words. She said, 'When will he be here?'

'He must have left as soon as he got your wire. He'll be in London tonight. He should arrive in time for the funeral.'

'All right. We must tell Arthur. I'll come down.'

Peggy switched the light off. 'Now, why would you? Just you try to rest a bit. I can hold the fort. Would you like some tea?'

'No. I'll be down in a little while.'

Her daughter went out, closing the door quietly, leaving her in the familiar room with her old things and her new things: the silver-backed brushes, a wedding present thirty-seven years ago from her uncle priest, and beside them a new pincushion doll sewed for her last Christmas by her eldest granddaughter. Her dead husband's shirts were in the dresser, his suits in the wardrobe, his slippers still under the big brass bed. Alone to grieve, she did not grieve. Since the death she had wept with friends who came to console her, wept when her children wept because she was a woman who, at the sight of a hearse, a neighbour's distress, a sad film, was quickly, meaninglessly moved to tears. But now, isolated from the contagion of other's sorrow, she thought of the death only as a background to this sudden homecoming of Michael, her eldest son. Flying home at last to father. Father. Wax statue face in the spare-room bed downstairs, a tape to keep the jaws shut, another tape to keep the shrouded legs from sprawling. Hairy knuckles laced in a pose of prayer, garlanded by the brown beads of a rosary.

At the family conference when her husband had the stroke, her other children had been against letting Michael know. Arthur, her second son, insisted his father would not wish it. Her daughters agreed, said the shock of their meeting might provoke a fatal anger. Besides, he was sinking fast. It might be too late.

But she knew what they could not. Years of lying in that bed taught her that Dan's hate was mixed with pride.

'The other day down at the yard, Christy Madden was pointing me out, take Dan Kelleher, our foreman, said he, there's a man with a son a doctor, and his eldest boy the head of a massive engineering company in America, all his daughters married to men with money. You know, said Christy, I remember his eldest boy, Michael, he was first in the whole of Ireland in his Junior Intermediate. Clever. Aye clever, said I to Christy, but a blaggard, an ungrateful blaggard. But it's true, he was clever, the lad, eh, Kate? Are you asleep, Kate? Oh aye, they never saw fit to make me supervisor, but never mind, I had my boys to point to. Eh, Kate?'

Besides, whether he wanted Michael home or not, hadn't she a right to see her son? Hadn't she? So, she

waited until all the children were gone and then, sitting
in the sickroom, she looked down, cold, God forgive her!
At that paralysed face and wrote out a wire, wrote it in
the way she knew for sure would bring Michael home.
Surrender. *I have a bad stroke and may not last. Can you
come? Father.* Looked at him, speechless on the bed, waiting his last end. What quarrel would not wither in the
sorrow of a son at his father's deathbed? And he, stubborn
hater, what else could he do but forgive?

But God did not wait for that. When she came back
upstairs He had reached out in His mercy and taken her
husband, leaving her only the body, crumpled up on the
bed like a thrown-off suit of clothes. Men and their quarrels. God had no time for that.

Quarrels, ah, she never knew the exact right of it, except
that Michael had been disrespectful about the clergy,
something he said in a debate his first year in university
that was repeated to his father in a pub a few days later.
Dan came home, furious, ordering him to go at once and
apologise. Michael refused, and so Dan hit him across
the face, calling him an atheist and a liar. Next morning
Michael was not in his bed. A week later, they found out
he was on his way to America. He wrote that he was sorry,
but his father did not accept his sorrow. For Dan, with age,
had become pious, preaching, praying, narrow, too narrow
not only for Michael but for the girls as well, complaining if
they went to dances, asking questions that (if he only knew
it) drove them out of the house and into marriages as fast as
they could find men to ask them. And yet, with all his harsh
talk, he held them, held them all. The letters Michael wrote

to her were secret letters to his father, his father who would grab them off her and tear them up unread. He was her son too, hadn't she a right to worry about him, hadn't she a right to hear? Hold your whist, woman, he would shout, as he threw the torn letter scraps on the fire.

These last years, the letters were fewer. Sometimes there was money in them, and he was not too proud to take that, stuff it in his trousers, saying it was owed to them. Her married daughters made excuses when she asked them over. In avoiding him, they avoided her. She saw it in their eyes: half pity, and a half contempt.

Oh Michael, he was always her favourite. Tomorrow, he will walk to her after sixteen years with never once a sight of him. What will he be like now? She tried to see his face but saw instead a passport photograph, the one he sent her when he went down to South America on some job. Someplace in the heat with a lot of black men, was it any wonder she was worried for that photograph face, for the son who wrote his little duty notes always with the same last sentence: *love to father and yourself, God bless, Michael.* But what, after sixteen years, did *love* mean?

Tomorrow she would know. Michael would be kind at least, he would help with money and Arthur would too, the children were good, they were a credit to her, every one of them. God had been good and her prayers for them had been answered. But oh! Looking down now as the street lamps blinked suddenly lit in the avenue, she felt alone, him dead, the harsh dialogue of thirty-seven years broken off for ever. Quiet in this dark-filled room.

After a time she drew the blind and switched on her

dressing-table lamp. The doorbell had been ringing: there would be new visitors downstairs. Maybe Arthur was back from the funeral arrangements? She put on her glasses, powdered her face, and went down, a tall woman, heavy breasted under her black morning dress, her white floss of white hair stiff as a guardsman's helmet. A widow, one day old, going to face condolence.

Old Canon O'Rawe pushed past Christy Madden in the hall, advancing plump, clerical, clean, and comforting as new goods. His pink, plump hands enclosed hers.

'Ah, Mrs Kelleher, I've just been in to say a mouthful of prayers, poor Daniel, God knows, a mercy, I hear he had little pain, when our time comes all of us, may we hope for a happy end, yes, miss him, many people will, a Mass I'm saying Sunday, not at all, the least I can do, nine o'clock Mass Sunday, yes, mustn't be keeping you now, not at all, not at all.'

Pink hands opened, releasing hers, plump, prompt retreat, skilled in saying the right thing and how could he mean one word of it, wasn't there one of his parishioners dying every day, what was he to Dan or Dan to him? He moved to the hallstand, picking out his neat black hat, his white silk scarf, leaving Christy Madden to speak his piece, advancing now with cornerboy strut, humorous horseface stiff with sympathy.

'Poor Dan, ah, Mrs Kelleher, Kate, I'm sorry for your trouble now. Sorry for your trouble.'

'Thank you, Christy.' (And is he drunk, I wonder?)

He gestured towards the back room, saying, could he go in now, did she think? To pay his last respects.

She nodded and followed as far as the door. Better keep an eye in case he . . . With her husband's old pals you could never be sure.

Christy hesitated in the doorway, then turned to her, hand shielding his mouth, a man giving a surreptitious tip on a good thing. 'Ah, now he looks lovely, now. Ah, you'd not believe it. Now I never seen Dan look better.'

Her youngest daughter, Maura, standing with Dennis Conneally, her husband, exchanged looks and giggles. But the other visitors in the dead man's room pretended not to hear. They eyed the Mass cards strewn about the dead man's feet, their heads bowed in prayer or mock prayer. Christy, unaware of his gaffe, moved towards the bed, stared with relish at the dead face, then knelt by the bed- side to mumble a Hail Mary. Mrs Kelleher kept her eyes from the face on the bed but waited, none the less. Get rid of him. Grief he pretends now, drunk and maudlin he'll be in an hour or two. Oh Dan, have a look at your best pal, will you? Have a look at them all, every chancer you ever took up with, every boozy, small-minded one of them.

Christy stood up, dusting his knees. 'I seen him last Tuesday, you know,' he whispered to her. 'And he was looking grand. Grand. No denying it was sudden. Sudden. Ah, we never know. We never know.'

His eyes strayed wistfully over her shoulder to the table in the parlour with its parade of bottles. Let him die of thirst, she thought. Was a drink all he came for? And will I ever see him again? Is this your best pal, oh manys the time, year in year out, what wee Christy Madden said, you told me. As if I ever cared one iota then or do now.

She let Christy out without asking him whether he had a mouth on him. She could hear her meanness told that night in some pub, and somehow this comforted her. Let them know at last what I think of them. But anger left her at the sight of Arthur, who came in and was hanging up his coat in the hall.

'How are you, Mama? We must have a chat. I've a lot of things to see to and a surgery at eight.'

That was Arthur. At times like this, a man, he followed the tradition, he assumed command. Although to her he was still a boy. Confusedly she remembered that from now on it would always be like this. Her sons would assume her husband's authority. She nodded and went back upstairs with him following. He looked cold, so she lit the gas fire in her bedroom.

'I've been down to the church,' Arthur said, 'it's all arranged. We'll move the body tomorrow night and the funeral will be at ten on Wednesday. I've been to Devlin's too and ordered six cars and a hearse.'

'Michael will be in time for the funeral then,' she said.

'Michael? Mama, surely you didn't send for *him*?'

'I did.'

Arthur looked angry. 'You never told me.'

She changed the subject. 'Who'll sit up tonight?'

'Dennis and Kevin,' Arthur said. 'I sat last night, and I have an early surgery in the morning. I'd sit again only I'm dropping on my feet.'

'I know,' she said. 'Yes.' So his sons-in-law would be Dan's last company at home. Dennis Conneally and Kevin Dunning, both mockers behind his back, they would wake him through this last night under his own roof. Because it was the custom. But would Dennis and Kevin grieve for him? She doubted it. They married the girls, not an old cantankerous railway foreman.

'If Michael had only arrived tonight,' she said. 'He could have sat.'

'Michael.' Arthur's voice was bitter. 'I doubt if Father would have been keen on that.'

'Och, what do you know?' she said. 'He was fond of Michael. He was fond of all of you.'

'Fond? For all Michael ever did for him?'

Jealous of each other. Brothers. And their father was jealous too, jealous of everyone else.

'Why did you send for Michael anyway?' Arthur said. 'I thought we agreed not to.'

'Because,' she said. 'His father would have wanted him here.'

'He never asked for him,' Arthur said sharply. 'Never.'

'How could he?' she said. 'When he couldn't speak.'

Tears surprised her at the memory of that dropped, speechless mouth. Why did Dan's hate live in all of them?

Her son was glad as a doctor for her tears; tears, he had learned, bring relief. He put his arms around her shoulders and pulled her towards him. 'Now, Mama,' he said. 'Now, Mama.'

But she wept, at last. Why had she blamed Dan when they were all of them the same, all haters, even she? Why had she cared more for them, her children, than for him? He had not been all she wanted, there had been times in their life together when the sight of him spilling his pipe ash on the carpet, sitting on the edge of their bed cutting his toenails, groaning about preferment, about others who had better luck, yes, there had been times, times too many to think of, when she had felt her heart stiff with hate for him, times lately when she watched him at prayer by his bedside, righteous as a pharisee, an old man full of hate and pride and caring for no one, not even her. Times, times . . .

But he was my children's father, he never did any disgraceful thing, his weaknesses were small and I knew them, I forgave them, I stayed with him. He did his best, what more could any wife ask, and he died in the state of grace, what more could any man want? And Dan, you came to our house years ago, I never think of that now, but no one had asked for me and I wanted you to ask and you did and I told my mother yes and oh Dan, I was glad of you, glad of you once, always glad of you. We had our life together, I was proud of the family we raised, we put up with each other for their sake, but I should be proud we managed that too, for it was not an easy thing for either of us. And now I grieve for you, only I am left to grieve, only I knew you, only I will remember, lonely I will be, the loss of you about this house, I must leave this house now for you never will, even though they carry you out tomorrow, you never will.

'Lonely,' she said aloud. 'I'll miss him.'

A voice said at the door: 'Dr Kelleher? Is Dr Kelleher there?'

'Yes,' Arthur said, getting up.

'You're wanted on the phone, Doctor.'

'I'll be down in a minute. Now, Mama, don't cry, we're all here. All the family. We won't let you be lonely.'

'Yes, dear. Go on down now.'

The family, ah, what can any of them do for me, children, children, none of you can take a husband's place. I never knew he meant that to me, I had my mind on you, all of you, educating you, feeding you, praying for you, bursting with pride that you all did so well for me, proud of the boy in America, the doctor, the sons-in-law, the grandchildren. And all these years I took him for granted, I never even saw him about the house, never thought of him, only for you children, children. And oh! yesterday, him lying in the bed with one side of him dead already, I wrote out that cable never thinking, thinking only of me, of Michael, a child I wanted to see again, cold to my husband, cold to his paralysed face, writing down what he could no longer stop me writing, taking from him the only thing he had left, his pride, his right to hate. And then, God forgive me, I remember going downstairs to send it and afterwards I went into the kitchen and ironed the sheets and pillowcases for the spare-room bed, knowing they would be needed soon. Only thinking of Michael coming, of the neighbours, of the house being tidy for death.

And when I came back upstairs, he was gone. His stranger eyes watching me from the bed, watching me as though for the first time he saw me, saw what I hid from him all those years. Saw me and left.

She raised her head, sobbing, her breathing harsh in the quiet of the bedroom.

'Oh, Dan. Come back, Dan. Forgive me.'

Frightened at the loud sound of her voice, she listened. Has anyone heard?

She switched on the table lamp. In the dressing-table mirror, her face, a road after rain, blurred, swollen, changed. Had no one heard?

No. She shook her head. No one.

Not even him.

UNCLE T

Vincent Bishop, standing at his hotel room window, saw in momentary reflection from the windowpane a nervous young man with dark eyes and undisciplined black hair. Above Times Square the sky haemorrhaged in an advertising glare. His reflection dissolved. He turned away.

'Are you nearly ready, Barbara?' he called.

She was in the bathroom putting polish on her nails. His uncle was due any minute. Maybe he should have bought a bottle to offer his uncle a drink before they started off? The half-dozen roses he had chosen for his aunt, maybe he should have taken them out of the box and let them stand in water for a while? Were half-a-dozen roses enough?

'Barbara, do you think I should run down to the lobby and get a box of chocolates?'

She did not hear him. Her and her nails. If this was the way she kept him waiting on the second day of their honeymoon, what faced him in the years to come? What would his uncle think of her? Or of him? How could he tell; he had never met his uncle. This morning, as soon as he and his bride checked into the hotel after the flight from Toronto, his uncle had been on the phone to invite them to dinner at his apartment. He was coming now to pick them up. He sounded very kind: but what could you tell from a voice on the phone? Of course, there was his letter. That was the important thing.

Grenville Press,
150 West 15th St.,
New York, 11, N. Y.

Dear Vincent,
    I am delighted to hear that you are planning to get married and that you are contemplating a honeymoon trip to New York. Both Bernadette and I offer our heartiest congratulations to you and our best wishes to your fiancée. Needless to say, we are looking forward to meeting you at last but, unfortunately, I cannot offer to put you up, as ours is a very small apartment. However, don't worry, I will find you a hotel room.
    I was most interested to read that you do not want to return to Ireland when your exchange teaching year in Canada is completed. I can well see the problems of going home with a new bride who is neither Irish nor Catholic and not likely to enjoy the atmosphere there at all. Now, as you also mention that you are fed up with teaching and would like to find something else, let me make you a proposal. How would you consider joining

*me here at Grenville Press? I'm sure that a young man
with your background would be ideal for the editorial
side of the business. As you know, Bernadette and I
have no children and we consider you very much a
member of our family. I might add that since I bought
out old Grenville's widow last year I am now the
proprietor of this firm.*

*Anyway, since you are coming to visit us in New
York, we can talk about this in more detail. In the
meantime, let me say that although we know each other
only from letters, I have long thought that you – a
rebel, a wanderer and a lover of literature – must be
very much like me when I was your age. I look forward
to our meeting. Till then,*

> *Affectionately,*
> *Uncle T.*

Uncle T. Three years ago, in Ireland, Vincent sat in his
bedroom sending letters over all the world's oceans, mes-
sages in bottles, appeals for rescue. *I am twenty-two years
old and have just completed an Honours English Language and
Literature degree at the Queen's University of Belfast. I am anxious to live abroad.* Resident's clerk in the Shan State, shipping
aide in Takoradi, plantation overseer in British Guiana – any
job, anywhere, which would exorcise the future then facing
him; a secondary school in an Ulster town, forty lumps of
boys waiting at forty desks, rain on the windowpanes, two
local cinemas, a dance on Saturday nights.

Back with the foreign postmarks, the form replies, the
We-Regret-To-Inform You's, came a letter signed *Uncle*

T. A letter in answer to Vincent's veiled appeal to a never-seen uncle who was now, Vincent's mother said, a partner in a New York publishing firm. The letter contained a fifty-dollar money order. The writer regretted that he could not suggest any job at that time but hoped that, relations established, he and Vincent would keep in touch.

They kept in touch. Even for a young iconoclast there was comfort in a precedent. And what better precedent than Uncle Turlough Carnahan who, like himself, had published poems in undergraduate magazines, who had once formed a university socialist club and who (again, like Vincent) had left his parents' house for ever after a bitter anti-clerical dispute? Vincent wanted to escape from Ireland. Uncle Turlough lived in America. Vincent dreamed of some sort of literary career. Uncle Turlough, by all accounts, had achieved it. Was it any wonder then that this relative was the one Vincent boasted of to his bride?

'Well, will I pass muster for the great man?' Barbara asked, coming from the bathroom, her nail polish still wet, her hands extended before her like a temple dancer's. She was small and fair and neat; her girlish dresses drew attention to her breasts and legs. They had met three months ago when she began to teach modern dance at the Toronto high school where Vincent was spending his exchange year. Since then, she and he had rarely been separated; yet they were strangers still, unsure of each other, too anxious to please.

'Pass muster?' he said. 'You'll do more than that.' He bent to kiss her ear as the room telephone growled twice.

'That must be him, Vincent.'

'Hello,' said the telephone voice. 'Are you decent? Can I come up for a moment?'

'Of course.'

The phone went dead. 'He's on his way up,' Vincent said.

'Oh Vincent, I'm so nervous.'

How could she be? What was Uncle Turlough to her, who three months ago had never even heard his name? Whereas he, for how many years had he dreamed that one day his uncle might beckon him into this literary world he dreamed of? How would she understand his panic now as he waited at the door of their room, remembering the slight, dark youth he had seen so often in his mother's photograph album, wondering how the person who now knocked lightly on the door would differ from that youth. Of course, those photographs would be thirty-five years old. Uncle Turlough must be almost sixty.

He opened the door.

'Vincent, how are you? Welcome to New York.' The stranger shook hands, then moved past Vincent. 'And this must be Barbara. How are you, my dear? Why, you're even more lovely than he said you were. Welcome, welcome.'

On the telephone Vincent had noticed it but had not been sure. Now, he was. The stranger's voice had no trace of his own harsh Ulster burr, but was soft, brogue, nasal, like the voice of an American imitating an Irish accent. Confidential and cosy, it told Barbara, 'Do you know, it's an extraordinary thing, my dear, but this husband of yours is the spitting image of me when I was his age. Look at us together. Don't you still see a resemblance?'

What resemblance? Vincent thought; but hoped Barbara would have the sense to pretend.

'Oh yes,' she said. 'Of course, I see it.'

The stranger bobbed his head in acknowledgement and as he did Vincent noticed his hair, black and shiny as a crow's wing, unexpected as the chocolate-brown overcoat and blood-coloured shoes. Resemblance?

'Do you have a couple of glasses, by any chance?' the stranger said, unbuttoning his overcoat to reveal a crumpled grey suit, too tight at the middle button. From his jacket pocket he took a pint bottle of whiskey and broke the seal. 'Bernadette won't be expecting us for a while,' he said. 'I left the office early. I thought we might have one for the road, here, before we start.'

Obediently, Barbara went into the bathroom, returning with two water glasses. 'I'd better phone for ice,' she said.

'Don't bother,' the stranger said. 'Just run the cold tap a while. There's no sense letting them rob you blind with their room service.'

He poured two large whiskies and presented them to his guests. 'I don't need a glass,' he said, raising the pint to his lips. 'It's bottles up for me.' Silent, they watched, their own drinks untasted. Then Barbara took the glasses of neat whiskey and went to run the cold tap, as ordered. If it were one of her relatives, Vincent thought, there'd be no surprise, the uncle would be just as advertised, solid, Canadian, safe, he would be the man he said he was and not – what? Oh Uncle, what uneasy eyes you have! What ruddy cheeks you have, Uncle dear!

'And how's your mother keeping?' the stranger asked.

'She's well.'

'Dear little Eileen, manys the time I've wanted to go home and see her and my other brothers and sisters and all the rest of the Carnahan clan. Maybe I will, some day.' He recorked the pint and put it on their dressing table. 'I'll just leave this here in case you youngsters need a little refreshment when you get home tonight. After all, it's your honeymoon.' He winked at Barbara who was coming out of the bathroom, a wink at once collusive and apologetic. 'Although you know, Barbara, my old mother used to say you should never give an Irishman the choice between a girl and the bottle. Because it's a proven fact that most of them will prefer the bottle. Am I right, Vince?' He punched Vincent's shoulder in uncertain good-fellowship. 'Now finish up that sup of drink and we'll be on our way.' Obediently, they drank their whiskies. Obediently, they got their coats and followed him to the elevator. At the lobby entrance the hotel doorman approached, asking if they wanted a cab. The stranger shook his head. 'You two wait here,' he said, and ran a block down the street to find a cab himself.

'*Well*,' Barbara said.

'Well, what?'

She made a face. 'I do not like thee, Uncle T, the reason why is plain to see.'

'What are you talking about?'

'Just look at him, Vincent. His hair, for one thing.'

'What about it?'

'Lovely head of hair,' she said. 'It's dyed.'

'Oh, come off it.'

'It's d-y-e-d,' she said. 'And I'll bet that's not the only phoney thing about him.'

'Now, wait a minute, what do you mean?'

'Darling,' she said, 'if he's a publisher, I'm Mrs. Roosevelt.'

'Now, give the man a chance, will you? Why jump to conclusions?'

She did not answer for, at that moment, a cab drew up in full view of the doorman and the stranger leaned out, beckoning them to come. In shame, they passed the doorman's contempt. *Give the man a chance* ... But as the taxi rushed them on to the bright carnival rink of Times Square, Vincent heard his father's dry, diagnostic voice: 'If your mother's family have a weakness, it's that never in my life have I known any of them spoil a good story for the sake of the truth.' Upgrading their relations, exaggerating their triumphs, hiding their shortcomings under a bluster of palaver, wasn't that what his father thought of the Carnahan clan? Even his mother, hadn't she a touch of it? When twenty-five exchange teachers had been picked to go out to Canada, hadn't she told all her friends the story as though her son was the only one chosen? And this stranger was his mother's brother. Could those letters about Grenville Press be Carnahan exaggeration? No, of course not. *Give the man a chance.*

'Your wife's an American, isn't she, Mr Carnahan?' Barbara asked.

'Yes, Bernadette was born right here in New York City, although she's of good Irish stock. Where do your people come from, my dear?'

'My grandparents came from England,' Barbara said.

'Both sides?'

'Both sides.'

And wasn't there a certain Anglo-Saxon attitude in the way she said that? But the stranger did not seem to notice. On and on he went, telling about the Tenderloin district, pointing out the Flatiron building, keeping the small talk afloat as though to distract his listeners from the true facts of the journey. For their taxi was moving from bad to worse, entering streets that Vincent would not have dreamed of in his afternoon of sightseeing along the elegance of Fifth Avenue, streets of houses whose front entrances looked like rear exits, of signs which proposed *Keys Made, Rooms to Let, Shoes Repaired.* A group of sallow-skinned men played pitchpenny on the pavement.

'Here we are,' the brogue voice said. 'It's very convenient you know, because it's right downtown.'

They skirted the pitchpenny players, entered the apartment building and climbed two narrow flight of stairs, their guide hurrying ahead of them to press a buzzer outside one of the corridor doors. He rang twice and as on a signal a woman opened the door, drawing a mauve woollen stole tight about her bosom as she met the corridor draught. To Vincent's surprise she was in her late thirties, a brassy blonde blown stout, wearing a grey sateen dress one size too small for her, moving her weight uncomfortably on tiny ankles and feet. 'Bernadette,' the stranger said. And kissed her cheek.

Those heads together, kissing, made Vincent think of

their mutual hairdressing problems. Did they dye each other's? Awkwardly he offered his gift of flowers.

'Oh, roses, aren't they lovely! Thank you, Vincent, aren't you the perfect gentleman! Barbara, dear, do you want to come with me and freshen up a little? Turlough, take their coats, will you?'

The sight of their overcoats disappearing into a closet reminded Vincent that the evening was a sentence still to be served. If only he had come alone to New York, if only he hadn't told Barbara that this job would be the end of their worries about what to do when his exchange year was over. If only – he thought of his father's remark – yes, if only he hadn't behaved like a Carnahan. And now, in confirmation of his mother's blood, the first thing he noticed in the living-room was a familiar face in an oval frame. Dyed hair or not, publisher or not, this stranger was his kinsman. The photograph was of Vincent's maternal grandmother. The living-room itself was strangely bare, its furniture worn and discoloured as though his uncle and aunt had several small children and had long ago given up the struggle with appearances. Yet the letter said there were no children. He looked at the bookcase near what must be his uncle's easy chair. Shakespeare, and some poetry, second-hand copies of Goethe, Swift, Dante, Dickens, Flaubert. All were dusty as though they had not been disturbed since the flat was first moved into. By a small table near a reading lamp were several well-used copies of *The Saturday Evening Post*. 'Glass of sherry?' his uncle said, coming in with a tray on which there were four glasses, none of them used. But the newly broken tinfoil seal of the sherry bottle lay beside them and the sherry bottle had already been depleted. Dark, uneasy eyes saw Vincent notice the diminished bottle level, skittered nervously towards the door as Aunt Bernadette reappeared with Barbara. Everyone sat down. Sherry was poured. The verbal gropings began. Aunt Bernadette brought out her wedding present (an ugly salad bowl) and was duly thanked for it. She asked about the wedding. Had they had a big reception? Had they sent photographs to Vincent's mother? How was she keeping, by the way?

'She's in great form, from her letters,' Vincent said.

'And your Dad, how is he? Turlough tells me you and your Dad didn't always hit it off too well. I hope you made it up with him before you came out here?'

Made it up? He had gone back to Drumconer Avenue the week before he sailed as an exchange teacher. His mother received him, talked to him for a long while, then asked him to wait. He sat alone in the drawing-room, listening for his father's step. He heard his father leave the surgery and go along the hall. His father did not come up. He went out of the drawing-room and looked over the banister. His father was at the front door, putting on his hat and coat.

'Father?' he said, 'Father . . .?'

His father did not look up. 'I have to go out on a sick call.'

'But couldn't you spare a minute? Or could I come too?'

His father did not answer. His father reached down into the monk's bench for his consulting bag. His father's attitude had not changed since that day two years before when he looked up from the breakfast table, the newspaper shaking in his fingers. 'So, this is your damn socialism, is it? Have you seen the paper? My son up on a platform at the university, helping a couple of Protestants to run down his religion and his country. *My son*. Oh, haven't I reared a right pup. You're going to apologise, do you hear? You're going to sit down this minute and write a public apology and send it out to this newspaper. Do you hear me? This minute!'

Vincent refused. His sister wept: she said his conduct had broken their mother's heart. His mother packed a suitcase and went on a pilgrimage to Lough Derg, walking in her bare feet over the stones of that penitential island, praying God to give her son back the gift of faith. But despite his father's rage, his sister's tears, his mother's penance, he could not recant. Oh yes, he loved them, he loved them all. But fourteen and eight made twenty-two, eight years of hypocrisy, of going to Mass and the sacraments for their sake. He had tried to tell the truth in that university debate. The truth troubled him. But his father belonged to a generation who had had their Troubles: they had no time for any others. And so, after a month of his father's silent anger, Vincent left home to become a schoolmaster in a provincial town. And two years later when he returned, hoping to see his father, his father reached down into the monk's bench in the hall, picked up his consulting bag and opened the front door leaving his plea unanswered. What answer had he wanted, he wondered? Forgiveness? Or merely some sign that they still were kin? They knew, both he and his father, that if he crossed the

Atlantic he might never return. But his father had to go out on a sick call. His father walked down a path, opened the garden gate, did not look back. Went down the avenue, turned the corner, no look back.

And now, remembering this, what should he say to his uncle's wife? What should he answer this strange woman who asked if he had 'made it up?'

'Ah, your father always was stubborn,' Uncle Turlough said, seeing his hesitation. 'I remember well. He and I were schoolmates—'

'Stubborn?' Aunt Bernadette said. 'But isn't it children that are stubborn when they go against their own parents? Don't be putting excuses into the boy's head, Turlough, you've no right. Look what happened with your own father. When you heard he was dead you sat in this room and wept.' She turned to Vincent. 'Too late to make it up then,' she said. 'Too late.'

Her face was very close. Her flabby, powdered cheeks were pitted and spongy as angel food cake. Yet a few years ago she must have been pretty enough to make an old fool dye his hair. A few years ago, before the fat, before the coarseness, before the skin began to sag as though her body had sprung a slow leak. An old man marries a pretty face and ends up in a room with a monster. Strange monster, what right have you to reproach me with my father? He turned from her, determined to ignore her.

She would not be ignored. 'Oh, I know you think it's none of my business,' she said. 'But Turlough tells me you're just like he was when he first came out here. So, I'm warning you, Vincent. Don't make his mistake.'

'Now Bernadette, now dear,' Uncle Turlough said. 'You're confusing two different cases entirely.'

'Am I? You never went home because you were too stubborn to go back on all your boasting. You were even ashamed of me.'

'Now, that's not true, sweetheart—'

'It is true.' She turned to Barbara. 'He's always complaining that I don't have his education. Well, I don't, but is that my fault? Oh, let me tell you, dear, your troubles are only starting when you marry into this Carnahan clan.'

'I can't believe I'll have any trouble,' Barbara said, smiling.

'Do you mean because you're better educated than me?'

'I didn't mean that at all, Mrs. Carnahan.'

'Oh yes, you did. But don't forget you're a Protestant. Show me the mixed marriage that doesn't have its troubles. You'll have your share of tears.'

'Drinks? Drinks, anyone?' Uncle Turlough said in a hoarse voice. 'Barbara, a little more? Vincent, can I top that up for you? Bernadette? Anyone and evenly . . .?'

No-one answered him. Barbara sat stiff in her chair, her eyes fixed on the lamp across the room. Aunt Bernadette, her neck red beneath the powder line, looked at Barbara in open dislike.

'Charity,' Uncle Turlough said, pouring himself the drink that no-one else had wanted. 'Charity for the other person's point of view, that's what counts. Don't try to make everyone else the same as you, that's the thing I've learned as I get older . . . Vincent, maybe you'd like to switch to a shot of whiskey?'

Maybe he would. Getting drunk might be the only way to survive this evening. So, Vincent said yes, aware of Barbara's sudden disapproval, watching her gather up her handbag as though she were preparing to walk out on him. In that moment he felt her Protestant prejudice against all the things which the words 'Irish Catholic' must bring into her mind: vulgarity, backwardness, bigotry, drunkenness. But the litanies of love he had recited to her these past three months, didn't they count for anything? Didn't she know very well that he was no longer a Catholic, that it was not his fault that he had been born Irish, that he could hardly be held responsible for relatives he had never laid eyes on? If her lovemaking last night meant anything more than animal desire, wouldn't she be suffering with him now, not sitting in judgement on him as though he had tricked her?

Still, he *had* tricked her, hadn't he? Tricked her by boasting of his publisher uncle, tricked her by holding out New York as bait knowing how bored she was with Toronto. Yes, he had. She knew it and she would make him pay for it. She stirred in her chair, turned towards his uncle and, in a disarmingly innocent voice, asked the question Vincent had feared all evening. 'By the way, Mr Carnahan, we've been wondering what sort of books you publish. Is it mostly fiction, or non-fiction?'

Aunt Bernadette looked at her husband. 'Fiction?'

'What about the dinner, dear?' Uncle Turlough asked. 'Isn't it nearly ready?'

'I'll go and see.'

In the silence which followed Aunt Bernadette's departure, Uncle Turlough poured himself another sherry.

'Well ...' he said. 'I thought Vincent and I would talk business tomorrow at the office. Tonight, let's just enjoy ourselves, eh?'

'Oh, I wasn't thinking of it in that sense,' Barbara said. 'I was just wondering if perhaps I've read some of your authors?'

'Authors?' Dark, uneasy eyes appealed to Vincent, found no support, fixed their gaze on a neutral corner. 'We – ah – we don't do any fiction, my dear. Not that I wouldn't be happy to do, mind you. But you see – perhaps I've never explained this properly in my letters – we're in a more specialised field.'

'Oh, really?'

Vincent stared at her, willing her to look at him. Drop it, can't you? But she had no mercy. 'Well,' she said, 'what sort of books do you do, then?'

'Books? Not too many books, I'm afraid. You see, we're not what you might call book publishers. We do a few directories. And we do brochures and booklets and pamphlets – that sort of work.'

'*Directories?*'

'Well, for instance, we do a dental directory, that's a very profitable line. We try to get out a new edition every five years. You'd be surprised how many dentists can afford to shell out five dollars for a nicely got-up book that has their name in it.'

'Dinner's ready,' said Aunt Bernadette.

Dinner. The fusty dining-room was crowded with heavy walnut furniture which, by the awkwardness of its presence, announced that their hosts did not often eat there. There was, however, a bottle of wine and the main dish of roast beef and baked potatoes was good and plentiful. A plated silver candlestick with three candles lit, and Irish linen table cloth still glistening new, its folds heavily creased from years of lying in a gift box, proclaimed that in honour of Vincent and his bride Aunt Bernadette had set out her best. But Barbara did not relent: the questions continued. Behind his uncle's apologetic smiles, behind the evasions, the unwillingness to be specific, Barbara laid the imposture bare; Grenville Press, those boastful letters notwithstanding, was in reality a hole-and-corner print shop whose main activity consisted of cooking up lists of names in the manner of a spurious *Who's Who*. There was, Uncle Turlough admitted, a great deal of work in canvassing people to get them to buy the books and brochures in which their names would be included, a great deal of 'sounding out groups in specialised fields to see if the response merits publication.'

'And what exactly did you have in mind for Vincent in all of this?' Barbara asked.

'Well ...' His uncle's dark eyes sought out Aunt Bernadette who sat silent, eating with a concentration which showed plainly how she had come to lose her looks. 'Well, I thought he might take Miss Henshaw's place. Eh, Bernadette?'

Aunt Bernadette nodded, still chewing.

'As a matter of fact, Vincent, the week you wrote to me saying you wanted to stay, that was the week we found out that Miss Henshaw had cancer of the bowel. She was our editor; my right arm, and old Grenville's before me. Wonderful woman, she could turn out anything you wanted, from a seed catalogue to a school prospectus. She was a great loss, but' –he smile painfully at Vincent– 'if it had to happen, then what better time than now, when it gives me a chance to offer you a good job with the firm. Which you'll accept, I hope.'

Barbara was waiting. He must speak. 'Well,' he said, 'of course, my teaching year isn't over yet. I haven't really made up my mind.'

'But you're fed up with teaching, your letter said.'

'Yes.'

'And you have to find some sort of job here, don't you?'

'Yes.'

'And you wrote that you'd like to live in New York, didn't you?'

'Yes.'

'Well, then?'

Vincent did not answer. 'I think Vincent was under the impression that you were a book publisher,' Barbara said. 'Book publisher? Book publisher. I see. So, you thought we were something on the order of Scribner's, did you? Something in that class. Ah, I'm afraid that's not the case, although who knows, great trees from little acorns, as the saying goes. Well, maybe it's my fault. Maybe I made the firm sound a little more important than it really is. But that's only human, isn't it? Isn't it, Vincent?'

Vincent nodded, his eyes on the table cloth. Aunt Bernadette, speaking for the first time since she had started eating, announced that she would serve coffee in the front room.

'Coffee, yes,' Uncle Turlough said, lurching to his feet, tossing his napkin on the table. 'Coffee it is. And we'll have a spot of brandy in your honour, children. Come along, Barbara, let me take you in.'

Coffee was poured. Aunt Bernadette took her cup and retired to the kitchen, refusing Barbara's half-hearted offer of help with the dishes. Uncle Turlough handed brandies around, then moved uncertainly into the centre of the room, his own glass held aloft.

'A toast,' he said. 'I mean, I want to tell you both how happy I am that you're here at last. I want to tell you how much tonight means to me. You see, Vincent, you're the first relative I've laid eyes on since the day I left Ireland. Yes, this is a great occasion. As you know, I've no children of my own and reading Vincent's letters was like living my own life over again. Funny, isn't it, how you and I have done so many of the same things? Yes ... so, *Cead Mile Failte* to you and to this lovely bride of yours and may this night be the beginning of your long and happy memories of New York.

Vincent raised his glass but Barbara put hers down. 'I'm superstitious,' she said, smiling. 'I never like to drink to something before we've really made our minds up.'

'Well, then, let's say, here's hoping,' his uncle said. 'Here's hoping you'll like it enough to stay. Eh, Vincent?'

'Here's hoping,' Vincent said, smiling in embarrassment. He and his uncle drank. Barbara did not pick up her glass. His uncle noticed that.

'As for money,' his uncle said. 'I think I'll be able to start you on more than you're earning as a schoolmaster.' He turned to Barbara, empty glass in his hand, in an attitude which reminded Vincent of a beggar asking alms. 'And you know, Barbara,' he said, 'if it's moving to a new place that worries you, Bernadette and I will do all we can to help you get settled.'

'It's not the moving that worries me,' she said.

'Then what is it, my dear?'

'Well, if you must know,' she said, 'I'm worried about the job and whether it's what Vincent wants.'

Said, her sentence hung in the air like smoke after a bullet. His uncle turned towards Vincent, waiting, his puffy face curiously immobile, his dark eyes stilled at last. In the kitchen Aunt Bernadette could be heard turning on taps, stacking dinner dishes. No one spoke and after a few moments his uncle pulled out his handkerchief and coughed into it. Coughed and coughed, bending almost double while Vincent watched, heartsick, waiting for the paroxysm to wear itself out, watching as his uncle straightened up again, handkerchief still shielding his mouth, eyes staring at them in bloodshot, watery contrition. 'Yes ... well, of course, that's for you and Vincent to decide,' his uncle said. 'Excuse me – this cough. Sorry. Anyway, it's my fault, talking business to a young couple on their honeymoon. *Mea culpa*. Now, let's talk about something else. How was your trip?'

'Very tiring,' Barbara said. 'I don't know about Vincent, but I feel quite exhausted.'

'Sorry to hear that,' his uncle said. 'If you're tired we

mustn't keep you too late. But it's still the shank of the evening, after all. Would you like another cup of coffee?'

'No, thank you.'

Again, there was a silence. 'Vincent tells me you teach modern dance,' his uncle began. 'I'm a great admirer of Katherine Dunham. Have you ever seen her troupe?'

'Yes.'

'And Martha Graham's Letter to the World,' his uncle continued. 'Yes, I used to go to a lot of ballet once upon a time.' He smiled at her as he spoke, smiled as though pleading for her friendship. But Barbara did not return his smile and so, rejected, he reached unsteadily for the bottle and poured himself another brandy. Vincent tried to speak; in that moment he felt embarrassed for this man who had written a letter, booked a hotel room, bought a festive meal, made a speech of welcome, and who, his illusion of family feeling destroyed, sat silent, half-drunk, his smile rejected. Vincent talked. He talked of the Abbey Theatre, of the plays he had seen in Toronto. For a few minutes, he and his uncle stumbled over broken rocks of conversation, recalling the sights and spectacles of former days. But a conversation with no dark corners could no longer be sustained. The talk died. Aunt Bernadette came back into the room to collect the coffee cups. Barbara gathered up her handbag.

'It's been a lovely evening, Mrs. Carnahan,' she said, 'and a wonderful dinner. But I'm afraid you must excuse me, I'm awfully tired from the plane trip. We had to be up so early this morning.'

Aunt Bernadette bent down, put the coffee pot on her tray, stacked the saucers, heaped the cups on top.

'Leave those dishes, won't you dear?' Uncle Turlough said. 'What's it matter?'

'I just want to put them in the sink.'

'But Barbara's leaving, dear.'

'I won't be a minute.' She picked up the tray, went out of the room and again they heard the rush of water taps. 'Bernadette won't be a minute,' Uncle Turlough said. 'She ... she likes to get the dishes done in one washing. I'll just go and hurry her up. Sit down for a second, Barbara. I'll be back in a moment.'

He went out.

'My God, Barbara, it's not ten o'clock yet. You could have been a bit more polite to them.'

'I didn't feel like it,' she said. 'I'm sick. Why didn't you have the guts to tell him? You'd be insane to take that job. *Insane*. Why didn't you speak up?'

'Shh! They'll hear you.'

'Well, what do I care? Do you think I want to spend our honeymoon being shown around by him, and that floozy of his? My God, Vincent - '

But at that moment, the sound of unmistakably quarrelsome voices reached them from the kitchen. 'I don't care,' Aunt Bernadette's voice said. 'let them go.'

'Ah now, wait a minute, sweetheart ...'

'Oh, shut up. I know you, it's your own fault, it's an old story, making yourself out to be something you never were.'

'Shh!' his uncle's voice pleaded. Mumbling, indistinct, the argument died to whispers. A door shut. Uncle Turlough came from the kitchen, his face fixed in its apologetic smile.

'We really must go,' Barbara said, standing up.

'Oh? Well then, I'll just run down and find a taxi for you. Just sit a minute, I won't be long, Bernadette ...? Bernadette, will you get the children's coats?'

In answer, the water taps roared again in the kitchen.

'Won't be long,' Uncle Turlough said, opening the apartment door. 'Vincent, get yourself a drink.'

The front door shut. Vincent stood up and walked towards the brandy bottle. He had drunk too much. He felt slow, uncoordinated, dull.

'Vincent, you're not going to have another drink?'

'I am.'

'I'm getting my coat then. Where is it?'

'In the closet in the hall.'

He heard her leave the room. He picked up the bottle. Perhaps in twenty years his face would bloat and blotch as his uncle's had. Drink, that was an Irish weakness. Self-deceit, that was an Irish weakness. He drank the brandy. He stared at the book-shelves with their dusty, unused books. Drunkenly, he turned to face his Carnahan grandmother on the mantelpiece. Never give an Irishman the choice between a girl and the bottle, she had said. Most of them will prefer the bottle.

The front door opened and he heard his uncle call: 'Barbara, let me help you with that coat. And is this Vincent's coat? I have a cab waiting downstairs. Where's Vincent?'

His uncle came in, his step unsteady, his face still fixed in that apologetic smile which was, wasn't it, the very

mirror of the man? 'Here's your coat, Vincent lad. And
wait till I get your aunt. Bernadette? Bernadette?'

He went out again and Vincent heard him go into the
kitchen. A moment later, the front door shut. Vincent ran
out to the hall. She was gone. Furious at her, he opened
the front door to call her back but, as he did, his uncle
returned from the kitchen. 'Oh, there you are,' his uncle
said. 'Bernadette asked me to say goodnight for her, she has
a touch of migraine.' He held out a clumsy parcel. 'Your
wedding present,' he said. 'I wrapped it up for you. Now,
what about a nightcap? One for the road. Where's Barbara?'

'I asked her to go down and hold the cab.'

His lie, complementing his uncle's, their mutual shame
as they stood face to face, each seeking to atone for his
wife's rudeness, each hoping to preserve the fiction of
family unity – Oh God, Vincent thought, we *are* alike.
Quickly, he opened the front door. 'No thanks,' he said.
'Goodnight, and thank you for a very nice evening. Don't
bother to come down, please.'

'No bother at all. But are you sure now, you wouldn't
stay a wee while? You could send Barbara home if she's
tired and then we could sit down over a glass, just the two
of us.'

'I'm afraid I'd better go. Barbara is waiting, you see,'

'I see,' his uncle said. 'Yes, of course. All right. I'll come
down and say goodnight to her.'

'Please, it's not necessary.'

'No bother,' his uncle said, following him out, pursuing
him down two flights of stairs, coming up with him into
the street. The taxi waited, its bright ceiling light showing

Barbara huddled in the far corner of the back seat. She did not appear to see them and Vincent, afraid that she would refuse to say goodbye, hurried ahead of his uncle and pulled open the taxi door. 'Say goodbye to him, will you?' he whispered.

'Where is he?' She looked past him, peering into the darkness of the shabby street. But his uncle had stopped about twelve feet from the taxi. She waved to him, and he raised his hand and waved back. 'Goodnight, my dear,' he called. 'Have a good rest.'

'Goodnight, Mr Carnahan. And thank you.' She smiled at him and leaned back in her seat. For her it was over; she wanted to go back to the hotel, to escape for ever from these people she despised. 'Come on,' she said. 'Get in.'

But as she spoke, Vincent heard a low voice behind him. 'Vincent? Vincent?'

Father, he had called. Father? But his father had not looked back. His father had walked down the path, opened the gate, no look back. Went down the avenue, turned the corner, no look back.

He turned back. There, half-drunk on the pavement, stood a fat old man with dyed hair. Where was the boy who once wrote poems, the young iconoclast who once spoke out against the priests? What had done this to him? Was it drink, or exile, or this marriage to a woman twenty years his junior? Or had that boy never been? What did this old man want of him now, Vincent wondered?

Forgiveness? Or merely some sign that they still were kin?

'Vincent,' his uncle said. 'I'll see you tomorrow, won't I?'

'Yes.'

'And Vincent? It's a good job, on my word of honour it is. I hope you'll take it, Vincent.'

'Well, I must think about it, Uncle Turlough.'

'Of course, of course. And Vincent, Bernadette, ah, you wouldn't mind her, some days she's not herself. I'm sorry you didn't enjoy this evening.'

'But we did. We had a very good time.'

'Thanks, Vince, thanks for saying that. Now, I don't want to keep you but I wish we'd had more time to talk. I know; you don't like the looks of the job. I think you don't like the looks of me, either. Well, I can't say I blame you, no, I can't say I blame you one bit. But, Vincent?'

'Yes, Uncle Turlough?'

'I was counting on your coming in with me. I had great hopes of passing on the business – but, never mind, if you don't want the job you don't want it and there's no use talking. Go on back now. You're on your honeymoon, you have better things to do than sit around at night with the likes of me. So off with you, lad, and good luck to you.'

'Goodnight, Uncle Turlough.'

As he shook hands with his uncle, Vincent looked at the taxi. There she sat, her pretty face averted in contempt. Was that all last night's lovemaking had meant to her? Didn't she know it was for both their sakes that he had come here this evening, that, unless he could find something to do on this side of the water, she would be condemned to a life of drizzling boredom as a schoolteacher's wife in an Irish country town?

He leaned into the taxi. 'Barbara, let's not go just yet?'

'I'm tired,' she said. 'I'm leaving.'

He fumbled in his trouser pocket. 'Here's your fare then.' He pushed the money at her and shut the taxi door. The taxi moved away from the curb. He watched: she did not look back.

'What's the matter, Vincent?'

He turned his face forming an apologetic smile, his dark, uneasy eyes searching his kinsman's face. 'I've changed my mind,' he said. 'Maybe I'll have one for the road, after all.'

'I knew it, I knew it,' said his spitting image.

LION OF THE AFTERNOON

The four non-professionals in the men's dressing room
wore blue blazers with white tin buttons in the lapels. On
the buttons, like a profession of faith, were their names and
the name of the Kiwanis branch they represented. All four
stared at Tait when he and his partner walked in.

Jack Tait was an achondroplastic dwarf, twenty-four
years old, with a handsome head and a normal torso, but
tiny arms and legs. His partner, Davis, was a melancholy
young man, six feet six inches tall. They were billed as
The Long And The Short Of It, and were to be paid
twenty-five dollars for this afternoon's work.

As Tait squatted on his tiny legs to unzip his overshoes,
a man wearing a magenta suit with silver lapels straightened up on the bench opposite and put a yellow balloon in
his mouth. He blew the balloon into a sausage shape until
it reached across the aisle and gently patted Tait's brow.
Tait looked up, smiling.

'Hi, Len. Haven't seen you around lately. Lots of work?'

Len let the yellow balloon deflate and stowed it carefully in his pocket. 'Been up to Kwee-bek City,' he said. His pronunciation of Quebec told the listening Kiwanis he was an American.

Tait stood on the bench, unbuckled his belt, and let his cut-down flannels fall, revealing thick, dwarfish thighs. 'How was it there?' he asked.

'Great, just great,' Len said. 'I had this one-week guarantee, see? But after the first night, the manager comes in with a contract for a full month. That's the good thing about this act, the jokes don't count. Just blow and smile. You see, this was a French audience in Kwee-bek. Worse than here in Montreal. None of them speak English good.'

'What club was it you were in?' one of the Kiwanis asked.

Len ignored the question. He turned to them politely. 'You in the show today?' he asked.

Four faces smiled as one. 'Yes,' one said. 'We're a barber-shop quartet.'

'Matter of fact, we've been a regular feature at this crippled kids show for the last five years.'

'Six years, Howie.'

'Yes, by gosh, it has been six years, come to think of it, Frank.'

'Say – what do you do with those balloons, anyway?'

Len obliged. He took a green balloon out, blew it up, then blew up a yellow one. Smaller balloons appeared and were inflated. With great dexterity, he began to bend and tie them. He held up a multi-coloured, balloon dachshund for the Kiwanians' edification.

'That's cute,' one said.

The others nodded. But, sidelong, their eyes were on Tait. He had dressed himself in baggy check pants, yellow blouse, and a comically cut, tiny tailcoat. He opened a box of paints and began to make up his face, white cheeks, wide clown grin, and star-shaped dimples. Childishly, he hopped down from the bench and began to shoo the Kiwanis away from the centre of the room. 'Would you mind?' he asked, his face serious beneath the painted grin. Curious, not knowing whether to smirk or look grave, they obeyed, instinctively dressing themselves against the wall in their quartet positions.

'Thanks, fellows,' Tait said. He turned his back and walked with dwarfish toddle to the end of the room. Then he ran towards them, little legs flying. Up he went and over in a forward flip, his acrobat shoes thudding squarely on the bare boards.

The Kiwanis were surprised. Being a dwarf was enough, they felt. What they had seen, the fact that he did somersaults, somehow lowered their stature. They were not athletic.

Tait, loosening up, walked on his hands for a moment. Then he did a standing somersault, leaping off the floor-boards like a trained terrier in a dog act. His partner, meanwhile, began to dress himself in a Superman costume, a black and white suit of cotton tights which clung to his lumpy muscles like shrunken underwear. Dressed, he took out a pocket mirror and began to comb his pompadour of black hair into a series of mounting waves, designed to make him seem even taller. Tait relaxed, flexing his fingers. Len carefully concealed his folded balloons in the pockets of his magenta suit.

Someone knocked on the door. Tait went to open, reaching up childlike for the door-knob.

'Hello, Shorty,' a woman's voice said. She looked over Tait's head into the room. 'Haven't seen Arnoldi, have you?'

'No, Doris,' Tait said.

'He was supposed to come in and help me,' she said. 'I'm all alone in that dressing room next door. Say - do me up, will, you, Shorty?'

She turned her back to Tait, dropping her rose dressing gown, revealing long, black-meshed legs, black-spangled hips. Her costume lay open in a deep V all the way down her back. Tait reached up, grasped the material firmly at the opening, and quickly zipped it shut, black spangles blacking out white nakedness. The Kiwanis looked at the woman and then at the dwarf. It was an interesting speculation.

'Excuse me,' a voice said.

'I'm sorry.' Doris hastily pulled her dressing gown up and moved out into the corridor. The newcomer bowed graciously. He entered the dressing room. He wore a grey hopsack suit and a white clerical collar.

'Hello there, gentlemen,' he said. 'Everything going all right, I trust?'

The Kiwanis, restored like fish to a tank of water, swam up at once to greet the minister, handshaking, talking. Tait backed into a corner and did some knee bends. Then he bounced over in a somersault. The minister was interested.

'Hard work, eh?' he said. 'Never could do that trick myself. Although I used to be a great man for gym. Yes.'

'It takes a lot of practice,' Tait said, stopping, looking serious.

'Keeps one wonderfully fit, though, doesn't it?' the minister decided. Then, slightly embarrassed – the little chap might take a remark of that sort amiss – he held up his hands for attention.

'Well, gentlemen,' he said. 'We have eight hundred crippled children waiting for us in our auditorium. They're all terribly thrilled and I'm sure we won't disappoint them. I say *we* because I'm afraid that you'll have to put up with me as your master of ceremonies.' He smiled headmasterishly. 'Now, we'll start with Tommy Manners, one of our local entertainers. The children love his singsongs. And after he's warmed things up, we'll bring on our friends the clowns, here' – he gestured at Tait and Davis – 'and then we'll follow with our singing quartet, and then the gentleman with the balloons, and finally, of course, the magician. Now, how does that strike everybody?'

'We're not a clown act,' Davis said. 'We're acrobats.'

'Oh, I see.' The minister looked at Tait. 'I thought the little chap here . . .?'

'So, we're on second, then. Okay?' Tait asked, hurrying over the rough spot.

'Yes. If that's all right with you, gentlemen.'

'But don't bring us on as acrobats neither,' Davis warned. 'Just leave the intro vague.'

'I see,' the minister said doubtfully.

As though on cue, a voice cried in the corridor. 'Ready there, Reverend?'

The minister opened the door. Outside, a very fat man was buckling an accordion against his heavy paunch. He stared into the room, his eyes finding Tait at once. As he and the minister went off up the corridor, his voice could be heard, asking: 'Who's the midget?'

The Kiwanis looked over at Tait. But Tait was using his eyebrow pencil, his clown face stony, unhearing.

A sound of accordion music drifted back from the stage. Then, gathering force, hundreds of childish voices faltered and followed the accordionist into a popular chorus. A tall man in evening clothes hurried into the dressing room, shutting the door, muting the singing sound. He took an empty pint bottle of whisky out of his tailcoat pocket, slid it under the bench, then opened a large trunk in the corner of the room. From the trunk he took a white, silk-lined cape, an opera hat, and a paper bouquet. He laid these on the bench. Then he removed several silk scarves, four metal containers, and a collapsible card table. He laid these on the bench too, placing them very close to Tait.

'Move over, Tiny Tim,' he said.

Tait turned, eyebrow pencil poised, clown face white and hideous. 'So, you're drunk again, Arnoldi,' he said. 'Doris will love that.'

Arnoldi aimed a mock blow at the dwarf's head. Tait jerked his head back. The eyebrow pencil smeared his cheek. He put the pencil down, then very deliberately scattered an armful of Arnoldi's scarves to the floor. He hopped off the bench, fleeing Arnoldi's anger.

'You little runt! So, you tell Doris I'm drinking?'

Tait dodged his head out from behind his partner's thighs. 'Tell her? She doesn't have to be Dunninger to find that out herself!'

'Arnoldi?' a woman cried.

'Here, here, stupid!' Arnoldi yelled, abandoning his pursuit of the dwarf.

Doris came in. She wore elaborate stage make-up and had removed her dressing gown. The Kiwanis watched her black-meshed legs and comely hips as she bent, picking up the scarves from the floor, folding them in a complicated layer arrangement. Arnoldi, ignoring her, carefully hid the paper bouquet in the pocket of his tailcoat.

'Acrobats?' a voice cried in the corridor. 'Acrobats next!'

Davis stood up at once, his head higher than the naked light bulb in the centre of the room. He picked up a fake bar bell and signalled to Tait. Tait toddled across the room and they went out together, the long and short of it. Single file they moved along the corridor, Tait close on his tall partner's heels to avoid having to push and tug at the church workers and Kiwanis officials who might not notice him, child-small in the crowd. In the wings they paused, waiting like wound-up toys.

'Look – about Arnoldi,' Davis said. 'I'll tell him to lay off you.'

'Who asked you?' the dwarf said angrily. 'Mind your own goddamn business.'

Rebuffed, the tall man looked out at the footlights.

Beside him, his tiny partner scuffed his feet, studying the stage for loose floorboards. Tommy Manners was finishing his act, the accordion shaking like a jelly cake on his huge paunch as he urged the children through a final chorus. He began to back towards the wings, panting like a tired dog, but the minister came out, leading him to the footlights for a bow, a long burst of applause.

When Manners finally backed off, his great rump bumped against Tait's forehead. He did not seem to notice but stood sweating and happy as the minister hushed the children's applause and announced the next act. When the minister had finished, Davis stepped out into the lights, rolling the fake bar bell carefully in front of him. The children were silent, their eyes on the strong man.

At centre stage, Davis bent double, his melancholy face contorted, his big hands gripping the bar bell, trying to raise it up. He lifted it about a foot, then falsely collapsed, letting it sink back to the floorboards. In the darkness, beyond the footlights, the children watched. Spastics, polio victims, the congenitally deformed: all knew what it was like to be defeated by the physically difficult. They waited, with the patience of experience, as Davis tried a second time.

In the wings, Tait raised his arms above his head and came out on a handstand, the ridiculous tailcoat rucked up his back, his silly clothes a Catherine wheel of spinning colour. Davis dropped the bar bell, ears pricked for laughter. It came. Tait, moving with an exaggerated, circus-dwarf swagger, walked to the centre stage, looked at the bar bell, rolled up his sleeves, picked the bar bell up, and twirled it above his head.

They were off then, off on a drum roll of laughter, into the hard work, the pratfalls, the somersaults, the running and the catching; awkward in spots where the adult hint of obscenity must be stripped from the routine, covering up by more outrageous antics than an adult audience would have stomached. And Tait, the children's favourite, commanded the stage. The curiosity, the smiles that met his every waking moment were assets now, turned to triumph by his willing acceptance of the dwarfish role. In the dark sea of the auditorium, the children's heads moved like weeds drawn back and forth by the tide of the tiny man's movements.

In front, close to the empty orchestra pit, were two rows of tightly ranged wheelchairs, attended by four white-uniformed nurses. In these chairs, mouthing and twitching soundlessly in an unpleasant parody of old age, the spastic children sat. When Tait, perched high on Davis' shoulders, fell thumping to the footlights for a final pratfall, nurses and children cowered back, on guard against familiar injury. But Tait bounded up, smiling, spat out a set of fake false teeth, waved at the cheering children, and went off on a handstand while the children made the auditorium shudder with their applause. Back he came to their frantic cheers, admired, a wonder man, the lion of the afternoon.

At the last bow, the hall lights bloomed and the minister stepped forward, hands raised in benediction on the cheering children. In the wings the Kiwanis waited, fussing with their bow ties, their minds already in close harmony as the acrobats passed them by. Tait lowered his head as he followed Davis along the crowded corridor. As always, he felt let down when, the act over, he was returned to normal stares. He dodged the patting hands of pleased officials, glad to reach the dressing room peace.

The non-professionals had gone. The professionals had taken over. Doris and Arnoldi sat side by side on one bench while Len, the balloon blower, drank from a bottle of rye.

'How was it?' Doris asked, with an angry side glance at Arnoldi, who had seized the bottle.

'Kid stuff,' Davis said. 'They'll go for anything.'

He sat down, tired Superman, on the bench beside Doris. Arnoldi drank, then passed the bottle to her with a malicious smile. Angrily, she took it, did not drink, but passed the bottle on to Davis. The tall man tilted it towards the ceiling as he drank, then lowering the bottle, leaned forward to hand it to Tait, who waited his turn, childlike, standing in front of the big people.

But Arnoldi, in a swift magician pass, flicked the bottle from Davis' fingers. 'Not for the louse,' Arnoldi said. 'This stuff is for people.'

'Go on, give him a drink,' Len said.

'It's my booze,' Arnoldi told him. 'And I say no.'

Tait turned away. He hopped onto the bench and began to scrub his clown face clean. Arnoldi put the bottle in his trunk then he and Doris began moving their magic props into the corridor. Davis sat silent, his great head drooping, as he watched his tiny partner change into street clothes: wind-breaker, ski cap, flannels.

'You in a hurry, Shorty?' he asked.

'Yes.'

'Wait, and I'll come with you.' He stood up, beginning to unbutton his Superman uniform.

'I don't want you. I got something to do downtown. I'll see you later at the hotel, okay?'

'Okay. See you later, Shorty.'

Tait went into the corridor. 'See you, Shorty,' Doris said. He did not answer. He went down the fire escape stairs to avoid the crowd and emerged at the back of the auditorium, pausing to look up at the stage where the Kiwanis rocked in humming unison. Moving behind the rows of watching children, Tait came to a door marked EXIT. He opened it and entered an ill-lit stone corridor, leading to the street.

'Wait! Where are you going?'

Tait turned. A woman, a tall woman wearing glasses, held the door open, calling him. She came out and put her hand on his shoulder. 'Looking for the washroom?'

'No,' Tait said. 'I'm leaving.'

She tightened her grip, guiding him further down the corridor. She opened a door. 'Wait here for a moment,' she said. 'I have something for you.'

Tait allowed himself to be pushed inside. He looked up at her face, wondering. She couldn't be that shortsighted. But then he saw the other small figure in the room and decided that with these particular children she might be excused her ignorance.

'Now, just wait here,' she said. 'I have to go and get it.'

She shut the door. The small boy swung around stiffly

to face Tait. His left leg was a withered miniature, supported by a heavy, stilt-like, iron brace. His features were bloated and coarse.

'I got a little car in mine,' he said.

Tait stared at him for a moment. Then asked: 'Did you see the show?'

'No, I got sick,' the boy said. 'Did you get sick too?'

'I was in the show.'

'Stupid,' the boy said. 'Only grown-ups are in the show.'

'Well, I'm – look, I can do a somersault,' Tait said, and did.

The boy watched him sombrely. Then sat down, stiff-legged, on the floor. It was obvious he had difficulty in standing up. Tait felt embarrassed.

'I can crack my knuckles,' the boy said. He pulled at his fingers.

Tait squatted on the floor beside him. He took the boy's hand. 'You have strong fingers,' he said.

'Want to feel my grip?'

They gripped hands and the boy squeezed. Tait made a grimace.

'You have big hands yourself,' the boy said. 'You should practice a grip like mine.'

'I will,' Tait said, seriously.

When the woman came back they were sitting on the floor, looking over the contents of the boy's gift package. She handed Tait a cardboard box, wrapped in green tissue paper. 'Now, this is yours,' she said. 'You can play with it here until the others are ready to go home. It won't be long.' She smiled at them. Tait kept his head down so that she could only see the top of his ski cap. When she had gone, he unwrapped the green package. Inside were a small rubber ball, a paper hat, a bag of candy, and a small metal automobile.

'Your car is better than mine,' the boy said.

'Here.' Tait held it out. 'You can have it.'

The puffy white face turned to stare. The weak eyes watered. Slowly, unsure of himself, the boy reached out and took the metal car.

'You can have the other junk too,' Tait said. 'Except the ball.'

'My name is Kenny,' the other said, watching Tait.

'Mine's Sh— Jack.'

'You're sure you don't want this stuff then. Only the ball?'

'Yes, just the ball,' Tait said. He put the ball in his pocket and picked up his club bag. The iron leg brace made a scraping sound on the floor as the boy turned, white, coarse face tilting upwards. The boy said, 'Why are you going away?'

'I better,' Tait said. 'I'm not supposed to be here. So long, Kenny.'

'So long. Thanks for the car and stuff.'

'That's okay.'

In the corridor outside three women were talking, their backs to Tait. They wore armbands marked OFFICIAL. Tait moved down the corridor in rubber-soled silence. He reached a steel door marked EXIT TO STREET. Opening it, he found himself at the top of a flight of steps. It was snowing and the street-lamps were lit. Across the street, a line of school buses waited for the children.

Tait paused at the head of the steps. He took out the rubber ball and looked at it again. It was like the one he had owned as a boy. The snow-whitened steps, the waiting school bus, the rubber ball: they touched on memories of his childhood.

He thought of the cripple on the floor. Remembered the iron brace, the tiny, withered leg. Did the leg never grow? It must be funny to be a cripple. How did they get in and out of bed, for instance? What happened to them if they fell in a lonely place and no one could hear them? Did women shrink from that tiny, withered leg?

Above him, the snow clouds had blackened to night. Like a baseball pitcher he wound his arm and skied the ball high into the darkness above. It fell, faraway, beyond the street lamps. Gaily, Tait ran down the steps.

FLY AWAY FINGER, FLY AWAY THUMB

This grotesque little story was told me by an old Sicilian whose face was brown and seamed like the bark of an oak, although his hair was as dark and as luxuriant as a young man's.

It is a weird story, indeed. Yet the narrator's manner carried convicton, even though he made no claim to first-hand knowledge. Perhaps it was the primitive atmosphere of that crudely furnished inn among the Sicilian mountains in which we sat which made reason capitulate. The firelight danced on the bare walls, the candles guttered, the four old olive growers listened and nodded. I was young, too – young enough to be carried by the sincerity in a man's voice.

This is the story he told me:

In the days of the briganti there were two men who lived in these mountains whose names were Salvatore and Luigi. This was before my time, you understand, and before my father's time. They were estate owners, neighbours, and Salvatore made much money out of his vines and orange groves until he fell a victim to the vendetta. Then his house was burnt down, his vines and orange trees were destroyed, his family was butchered. And he himself would have perished had not his neighbour, Luigi – a brave, simple man who owned only a few poor vines – hidden him in his house until the danger had passed.

Salvatore, however, had friends. He took to the hills, and there he formed a powerful band of outlaws, led by himself, with Luigi as his right-hand man.

But times were bad. There were then too many outlaws in Sicily for brigandage to be a profitable occupation. You can imagine, therefore, how Salvatore and Luigi were when they heard that a rich troupe of entertainers had come to Sicily and were then playing in Messina. It was said that these performers, whose leader was a conjuror called *Il Potentato*, the potentate, wandered around Europe and made money by their performances or by any illegal method which came their way. The greatest criminals they were, those performers! Why else should they come to Sicily if not to take refuge where they could not easily be found? Moreover, it was clear that they intended to remain for a long time.

'If they are to stay a long while here in Sicily,' said Salvatore, 'they must have much money with them. Is it not true, Luigi?'

'Certainly it is true, Salvatore.'

'And if they stay here a long time, will they not steal much more money?'

'They will, indeed. There can be no doubt of that.'

'They will steal money, Luigi, from our poor country-men, who are already so greatly afflicted by bandits that they can ill afford to lose money to foreigners as well.'

'Indeed, you are right, Salvatore!'

'Should we not, then, benefit our countrymen by reliev-ing these strangers of their wealth, so that they will have to return to Italy or France, where they can make more money out of their entertaining?'

'Yes, Salvatore, we should if that is possible. But this man, this conjuror, *Il Potentato* – he must be a clever man—'

'Santa madre! It is true that he must be clever with his hands – to say "Ecco! Here is a rabbit where there was no rabbit." But he cannot turn us all into rabbits. Luigi. He is a conjuror, not a magician.'

This discussion took place in the heart of the moun-tains, in the stronghold which Salvatore's band had made for themselves among the rocks and caves. It was deter-mined forthwith to send two men, the very next day, to learn what they could about *Il Potentato*.

A few days later they returned. 'He is a man,' they said, 'at whom you cannot help laughing as soon as you see him. He has a white face which changes all the time as if it were made of putty, and his lips are thick like a negro's. He makes great fun of himself, and his friends also make fun of him – but when he tells them to do a thing they do it. We went to see him and his company give a performance, and *Il*

Potentato put on a black robe and a pointed hat with moons and stars on it. He looked very mysterious then, but that was because he wore a black mask and a white beard. When, at the end, he took off his mask and hat and beard, everyone roared with laughter to see what a poor thing he was.'

'Did he make rabbits appear?' asked Luigi.

'He did many wonderful things. He made rabbits and frogs; he turned water into many colours; he sawed a woman in two halves, and yet each half was alive and felt no pain.'

'All that was trickery,' was Salvatore.

'Yes, it is true that it was all trickery. We have heard of these things before, although we have never seen them until now.'

'But when he is not performing,' asked Salvatore, 'what then?'

'Ah! There is a woman whom he goes to see in Milazzo – a woman named Maria Sganarelli. Gian here went to see her and made love to her.'

'She did not wish me to make love,' said Gian. 'She told me she already had a lover. I think she was afraid of him.'

'But he goes often to see this woman?'

'Many times. Sometimes there is a friend with him and sometimes he goes alone. Always he goes on horseback.'

'Amici,' said Salvatore, 'tomorrow night, or the next night perhaps, Signorina Sganarelli will wait in vain for her lover to come.'

The next night, Salvatore and Luigi helped themselves most skilfully and so made it easy for Heaven to help them too. They had to wait only for a little while before *Il Potentato* approached on his way from Messina to spend the night at Milazzo. He was surrounded and politely bidden to dismount. Then his hands were tied behind him, he was set on his horse again and led up into the mountains, between the horses of Salvatore and Luigi. There is no need to tell you that he was guarded very carefully, so that he might not escape by means of any conjuring tricks.

When he was once more inside his stronghold, Salvatore sent for his prisoner and looked at him for a long while before he spoke. He was indeed a strange man, *Il Potentato*. His nose turned up and his face was as if it were made of rubber. He had long, slender fingers like a woman's, and he clasped them together while he waited for Salvatore to speak. Then a little white mouse ran out of his pocket and climbed his arm. He apologised with a smile, put the little mouse in an empty pistol holster, and, after shaking the holster three times, returned it to its hook on the wall. Salvatore looked inside the holster and the mouse was gone.

Salvatore, however, took no more notice. He told the conjuror that he wanted money, much money, and that he must write a letter to his friends, telling them to bring 100,000 lire to a certain place at a certain time. Otherwise, *Il Potentato* would be killed. That was impossible, said the conjuror, for he could not write.

'Very well,' said Salvatore. 'I myself will send your friends a message, and they will know by your absence that what I say is true.' That also was impossible, said *Il Potentato*, for he must return to Messina the next day in time to give a performance. 'That shall not be,' Salvatore replied. 'You shall not leave here until I receive my 100,000 lire.'

Luigi took the conjuror away and locked him up. There was no danger of him escaping, for the room in which Salvatore and Luigi kept their prisoners was hollowed out of the solid rock. It had a heavy iron door in which there was one small peep-hole, and this door was secured by a lock and two bolts. Not even a conjuror could perform the impossible.

This night there was already a prisoner in the cell when *Il Potentato* was brought there. Paolo was the name of the other prisoner. He was a member of Salvatore's band, who was being punished for trying to steal more than his share of plunder. He was an indolent man and was not greatly unhappy at being a prisoner.

A few minutes after the door had closed behind the new prisoner, Paolo prepared to blow out the candle which, apart from a quantity of straw, was the only furniture of the cell.

'Wait!' said *Il Potentato*. 'You have a knife – is it not so?'

'Yes,' said Paolo. 'But how - ? '

'Because I see you have scraped a hollow in the ground for your hip-bone. Lend me your knife.'

Paolo thought he could be trusted and lent him the knife. 'But it is not a throwing knife,' he said. 'And the peep-hole is not large enough to throw a knife through it.'

'Grazie,' said *Il Potentato*. 'I do not need a throwing knife.'

Then he spread out his left hand on the ground before

him, and he cut off the first finger and the thumb. Taking a handkerchief from his pocket, he wiped the blood from the knife and restored his property to Paolo, thereafter using the handkerchief to bandage his mutilated hand. He went to the door and looked through the peep-hole. Paolo knew there was a guard posted a little way along the passage, but this guard, it seemed, was not looking at the door, for *Il Potentato* took his two severed fingers and dropped them out through the hole.

'It is time to sleep,' said this strange man; and, after blowing out the candle, he lay down on the straw and fell soundly asleep.

For Paolo sleep was out of the question. He lay staring at the doorway and watching the round hole grow brighter as his eyes grew accustomed themselves to the darkness. After a while, the hole flickered and became very dim – the guard's candle had gone out. It was a little while after this that Paolo heard a faint clicking sound – such a little sound that even his own breathing rendered it inaudible. Yet he was sure he was not mistaken. He rose and went to the peep-hole.

Save for a shaft of moonlight the passage was in darkness. At the far end Paolo could see the guard sitting with his back against the wall and his head lolling on his knees. He was fast asleep. And then, in the blue beam of moonlight, Paolo saw something else which made his knees shake so violently that they knocked against the door; for, on the moonlit ground, he saw a finger and a thumb painfully dragging a key, which emitted a slight metallic, scraping sound.

Paolo blundered back to his corner and buried himself so deeply in straw that only his eyes were uncovered. From time to time his ears caught the faint clink of metal – almost inaudible at first, but then louder as if the key were being dragged up the outside of the door. There followed a different kind of scraping – the key, he thought, being slowly turned in the lock. Then there was a sharp click, and after that the iron squeak of a bolt being drawn back. After this squeak had been repeated for the second bolt, there was silence.

Soon the straw rustled and told Paolo that his fellow prisoner had woken up.

'Amico,' he heard him whisper, 'you are awake.'

'S-sí,' replied Paolo.

'Then come with me. You are free to depart.'

'I will stay,' said Paolo.

'Very well, if you wish. In that case, I can leave a message with you. Tell your bandit chiefs that I intend to teach one of them a lesson. Tell them also that when *Il Potentato*'s flesh is severed, a soul is cut off from earth.'

He then went softly to the door and passed out of the cell. The last Paolo saw of him was his figure silhouetted against the moonlight as he picked up his finger and thumb and put them in his pocket.

When they heard this account next morning Salvatore and Luigi whispered many times the phrase 'I intend to teach one of them a lesson.'

'He will teach one of us,' breathed Luigi, '*by killing the other.*'

That they believed Paolo's story, strange though that

story was, is not surprising. They knew there was no normal means of escaping from the cell. Moreover, they found a little blood on the cell door and a trail of red drops leading from the doorway to the guard's seat. On that seat they found the guard's dead body – strangled, with his pistol in his hand and in his empty holster a little white mouse.

Madre di dio! What a change one conjuror made in those two men! They dared scarcely eat or sleep or venture out of their stronghold for fear of – for fear of they knew not what.

'It was all trickery,' said Salvatore. 'He cannot harm us here.' Yet he did not believe what he said, nor did he convince Luigi.

It was their custom to keep sentinels posted at strategic points on the mountain-side. And one day two of their men brought to them a stranger whom they had captured as he rode up from the valley. This stranger gave his name as Enrico, and said he was a native of Ragusa in the south.

'A man,' he said, 'has paid me a large sum of money to come to you here and pay you the ransom which he said he owed you.'

'What is his name?' demanded Salvatore.

'His true name I do not know,' replied this man Enrico. 'But here in Sicily people call him *Il Potentato*. He is a conjuror from foreign parts. The ransom, he told me, is contained in this box. But I have carried the box for three days and three nights, and it seems to me that there is something inside it which lives. Sometimes you may hear it scratching. For fear it should contain a snake, I advise you, my friends, to be careful how you open it.'

Salvatore and Luigi looked at the little box that was no bigger than a man's hand and was tied most neatly with green ribbon.

'This man,' said Salvatore, 'this conjuror – had he – had he a bandaged hand?'

'It may have been so,' replied Enrico. 'I could not tell, for he was wearing gloves. On both his hands he wore gloves, although the weather is warm.'

'Luigi,' said Salvatore, 'we must burn this box. We will go to the charcoal burner's hut and we will burn the box. Pick it up, Luigi, and come with me.'

Luigi, however, would not touch the box. Salvatore called him many hard names for his cowardice, but he would not touch it either. So in the end they ordered one of their men to take the box, and then they all went, the three of them, to the charcoal burner's hut and stood in a ring around the brazier.

'Drop it in,' commanded Salvatore.

The man took the box, holding it by the emerald-green ribbon, and let it fall into the heart of the fire. There was a faint knocking sound as it lay in the flames, and that was followed by a hissing and a spluttering. They watched it until it was consumed, and then they rode back to their stronghold. Their hearts were lighter on the return journey, you may be sure, than when they had ridden forth. Their hearts were lighter, indeed, than they had ever been in their lives.

'Now,' said Luigi, 'we are safe.'

'Yes,' said Salvatore. 'Praised be the blessed saints! We are at last safe.'

The man Enrico asked their pardon when they returned, and said he had wished them no harm. Indeed, it was he who had warned them about the box. The journey back, he said, was a long one, and he wished to stay the night if they would let him.

Salvatore and Luigi said he could stay if he wished; but they were not fools – he would have to be content with being locked in the cell. Then, when he had been locked up for the night, they caroused with their men until a late hour, and at last went to bed.

In the morning, when Luigi arose ... But, Signore, I can see you know what Luigi found when he arose. He found his friend, Salvatore, quite dead – strangled, his eyes staring as if he had seen something horrible when he died, his tongue protruding from his mouth. On his throat were four marks – the impression of two thumbs and two index fingers. There were a few drops of blood on the ground beside him, and the trail of blood led to the cell door which was open. The guest, Enrico, had of course gone, leaving behind him nothing but a little box, the size of a man's hand, beside which lay a strip of ribbon – red ribbon. The inside of the box was stained with blood.

OFF THE TRACK

The Coles left their taxi on the highway and walked into the village. The side road, rutted with heavy folds of dried mud, was proof, Margaret said, that few cars passed here. Alex agreed. In mild excitement he and his wife quickened their pace.

Alex Cole carried a Rolleiflex around his neck and a light meter stuck like a watch fob out of the pocket of his white shirt. Margaret wore a bright straw hat purchased in a tourist shop in Port-au-Prince. Ten days of the summer tropics had warmed their Northern skin to a painful blush. But still, they were not, they felt, just tourists. For two years they had taken summer classes in French at the University of Toronto in preparation for this trip; they had read several books on the history and more of the island and Alex, a sociologist, hoped to deliver a lecture on Haiti when he returned to Canada. Which was why the camera, they explained. Alex hoped a few pictures of the subject might help illustrate his talk. Which was why, in a way, this search for a village off the tourist track.

The village began by signs. A one-storey house, smeary yellow, with a corrugated iron roof. Some chickens in a fetid garbage dump. A second house, a few yards farther up the road. Then, multiplying, the trailing entrails of the place: women in bright bandannas moving barefooted from sun to shade in unidentifiable household tasks; a gaggle of bare-bottomed children sailing stick-and-paper boats in a muddy gutter.

Alex Cole passed these children slowly, daring himself to stop, take his time and two differing exposures. But the children crouched in pretended busyness until the stranger's shadows had fled to the long gutter. Their quick eyes turned then, watching the two *blancs*, the young woman who walked so easily in shoes, the young man who stared from right to left as though he had lost his way. The children watched the *blanc* backs grow small in the distance and then, with nothing said, went back to sailing home-made boats down gutters.

Forgotten, the Coles had also forgotten the children. For here the village became two rows of long huts behind low fences of leaved bamboo. In the open doorways, easily visible from the road, whole families could be seen in thick community.

'More like it,' Alex said. Margaret nodded. They kept their conversation at a minimum, partly from a fear of seeming to comment on the villagers, partly from a feeling of intrusion. The Coles, as Canadians, prided themselves that they, unlike Americans, were free from any colour prejudice. But the sounds, smells, and colours of Haiti made them vaguely ill at ease. Engrossed with unobtrusive looking, they did not notice the approach of an old peasant woman, persistently switching the rump of her burro steed as she forced it off the crown of the road to make way for the *blancs*. But as she passed they looked up at her, smiling and nodding to show their friendship. The old woman's surprised, head-over-shoulder stare was further proof that not many tourists came this way.

Again the Coles exchanged meaningful nods. They felt like medieval travellers arriving at some long-awaited destination. There was an achievement in this discovery, negating the disillusions suffered in ten days of diligent but dispiriting search, disillusions which Alex had summed up over after-dinner drinks the previous evening as 'the let-down of the normally abnormal.'

Haiti was, as the histories promised, a Black Republic. Its people were, as advertised, happy and seemingly free from any racial antagonism towards the white stranger. The island was beautiful and if Port-au-Prince was a giant slum, it was, Alex said, a slum of the Haitians' own contriving. Even the hints of undemocracy in the luxurious villas of police and government officials were, they agreed, the sort of normal abnormality one might expect in a country founded by slaves who later transformed themselves into kings and queens. And not, Margaret added, any particular business of theirs.

What was their business, and a depressing anti-climax to the long voyage from Canada, was the evidence of a painful native desire to make Haiti seem like any

other tourist centre. The kidney-shaped swimming at
the Coles' hotel was an affront. It, like the empty peel-
ing International Trade Fair Pavilions (shades of the
Canadian National Exhibition!) and the voodoo ceremony
at which the Coles sat in uncomfortable proximity to
eighteen other tourists at what appeared to be a drunken
barn dance, was exactly the kind of thing the Coles did
not pay their hard-earned money to see. The last thing in
the world they wanted was a guided Cook's Tour, a hotel
with American bathrooms, a hint of home. They were,
they admitted, just a trifle disappointed.

But now, before them, was an end to all that. The village
street dissolved without warning into a stony, irregular
square, large as a stadium, fenced by high old houses, two
gimcrack stores and a large, recent building which housed
a public market. The Coles broke silence in a mutual
murmur of pleasure and moved towards the market for a
closer survey. Live chickens scuffed and scratched in wire
cages. Men in Panama straws and faded shirts paraded
up and down the narrow alleys of the place, looking and
touching, commenting in loud *creole* shouts of interest
and disparagement. In front of the building, on a narrow
strip of concrete, old men and women sat patient under
the sun's glare, offering undistinguished bundles of cloth
to a few passersby. All turned to watch the *blancs*. Brown
faces, quick with curiosity, appraised the camera, admired
Margaret's shoes.

'Times Square,' Margaret said. But their arrival
brought a gradual quiet. The noise in the market building
had diminished. One of the stores was shuttered and on

a low balcony under the corrugated iron awning of the second, a few elders smoked in watchful calm. The Coles made an aimless circuit of the square's perimeter, then stopped, uncertain.

'If only I could get some candid shots,' Alex said.

Margaret, noticing his indecision, swiftly resolved it. 'Look. Supposing we walk by that market again? I'll pretend to pose and when you've got it in focus, I'll step aside a little and you can photograph those old clothes-sellers behind me.'

Alex agreed. He was new to all this and nervous. He envied but did not admire the gall of professional photographers. And so far, he had not had much luck. Even the most insensitive tourist was aware that Haitians waved off any camera pointed in their direction. Something to do with voodoo, one of the hotel guests said. Alex did not believe this. These people had a natural human dignity. They resented being treated as colourful animals. But he wanted pictures. Yesterday, he had failed, after stiff glares and jabbered warnings, to capture the old fruit-sellers in the Port-au-Prince market. If he could get some pictures here, they would illustrate this visit, this walking off the track into the heartland.

So, he followed his wife towards the marketplace, watching her station herself in front of the clothes-sellers, remove her straw hat, smiling as she shook her sleek fair hair back on the nape of her neck. He peered into the ground-glass window of his camera, focussing on Margaret's profile, then moved the camera slightly to the left to bring his real subject into the field of vision. But the clothes bundles were abandoned. The vendors had quietly moved out of camera range and now stood watching, half-invisible in the shadows of the market building. There was nothing left to do but take Margaret's picture. He made a small motion of failure and cranked his camera up to the next exposure.

'Shy, do you think?' Margaret looked back at them ready to smile the moment any greeting or curiosity was offered. But the dark faces studied stony ground.

'Let's not force it,' Alex said. 'If they've never *seen* tourists, it'll be even worse than Port-Au-Prince.'

'I could try asking them—'

'No.' He closed the camera case ostentatiously, took Margaret's arm and walked her to the centre of the square. He noticed that the villagers did not return to their bundles.

'I wish I'd never bought this damn camera,' he said.

'But darling, you *did* buy it. It's ridiculous not to use it.'

He lit a cigarette, forgetting to offer her one. She reached brusquely for the pack. 'Well?' she said. 'What next? I mean, why don't you let *me* ask them?'

'No.'

'So?'

'So, I'll take an overall shot. And then we might go to that store place. Maybe we can get something to drink there.'

'Honestly,' she said. 'You make everything so difficult. They won't eat you, you know.'

His hands fumbled with the camera case. He walked to the exact centre of the square and took a picture, aware that all he had was stony foreground and a low shed. A waste. He shut the camera once more and went back to Margaret. In silent anger they walked towards the low balcony where the elders sat under a sign that said simply *Magasin*. The elders, four old men in cane chairs, turned severally to glance behind them at the loose, fly-screened door of the store, as though wondering what the *blancs* could possibly want there. This had the effect of slowing the Coles to a standstill.

'Will we go in?'

'I don't know,' Alex said. 'I wonder.'

'Well, let's not stand here.'

'*M'sieu?*'

The little boy was about ten years old. They had not seen him come up. His smiling brown face was smudged with white dust as was the ragged yellow shirt he wore. His shorts were oversize and patched, bunched against his narrow stomach by an end of sisal rope.

'*M'sieu?* Photo? Me?'

The Coles looked at each other, their anger draining in swift gratitude. Slowly, their smiles paralleled that of the child.

'Let's make a portrait of him first,' Margaret suggested. 'And then you can use him, you know, maybe for that old-clothes shot. He could sit by one of those bundles.'

'Photo, *ça va?*' the boy asked.

'*Oui, oui.*' Margaret touched the boy's dusty head with her fingers. '*Très bien. Monsieur va prend ton photo, de suite.*'

'*Bien.*'

The child smiled as Alex put a light meter close to

his cheek, and kept smiling as Alex made three head-and-shoulder shots. Afterwards, they led him across the square, sitting him down beside one of the abandoned clothes heaps. Readily, he caught their meaning and held up a length of cloth as though offering it for sale. Margaret laughed, the boy chatted in unintelligible *creole* and Alex, composing and focussing, found he had shot twelve pictures and must change the roll. He looked around for a shady area to unload his camera.

'What about that store place, darling?' Margaret suggested. 'Perhaps we can get that cold drink, now?'

Alex looked dubiously at the boy. 'And our subject?'

'*Tu vas rester içi une petite minute,*' Margaret told the boy.

The child's smile failed. Immediately, he came close, dusty palm extended.

'Cigarette, *M'sieur?*'

'He's too young to smoke,' Margaret said.

'Wait.' Alex took a quarter from the change in his pocket and out it in the boy's hand. 'Here,' he said. 'Now stay here, okay?'

'Okay.'

The four elders nodded stiffly but politely as the Coles mounted the balcony steps and pushed open the door of the store. A bell rang in the shadowy room within, warning of their arrival. But the fat black woman who waited behind the counter had, they sensed, been expecting them ever since they entered the village. Margaret asked for something cool. The woman nodded and produced two dripping, warmish cokes from an ancient icebox under the window.

On the store counter, unnoticed at first, was a revolving rack of postcards. There were the same views on sale in Port-au-Prince and Petionville.

'Just look at this,' Alex said. 'Someone's been here before us.'

But Margaret, jealous of their discovery, would not allow it. She fingered the cards pointing out that they were dusty and few. 'Why, no one's touched them for ages,' she said. 'Anyway, I'm going to ask this woman. She'll know.'

The woman, hearing the question put in French, nodded and smiled in a way the Coles had learned meant incomprehension. They would never know, Alex said. But Margaret tried a second time while Alex went to the darkest corner of the store to reload. He was winding the transport crank of the Rolleiflex when he heard the first scream.

'Oh, my God,' Margaret whispered. 'What's that?'

Whatever it was, it was in the square outside. Alex left the camera on the counter and ran to the screen door. As he narrowed his eyes to stare into the sun, he felt Margaret's finger-nails digging into his forearm.

'Do something! *Do* something; Alex!'

In the square a man was thrashing the boy they had photographed. The man had taken off his heavy belt and as the Coles watched, he spun the child slowly in a semi-circle, his left arm whirling the belt in a wide arc. The belt hit the boy's body with a sound like tearing cloth.

'Stop him, stop him!'

Alex felt his wife's hands pushing him onto the balcony. The screen door banged shut behind him. Slowly, the row of elders stirred in their seats. The nearest, his neck wattled like some ancient turtle's, a flap of skin falling over the collar of his salmon-pink shirt, turned his head sideways and upwards to look at the *blanc*. He put a narrow cigarillo against his teeth and a thin stream of smoke floated towards Alex's face. The man in the square raised the belt. Again, Alex heard the tearing sound, the stiff, boyish scream. But did not move.

The punisher wore some sort of uniform; faded suntans, a soldier's cap. A policeman? Or the boy's father? As Alex stared, uncertain, the belt flew again, again it fell. Yet he could not move. He stood silent on the balcony, a few paces from the elders, as the punisher delivered two more strokes. The boy fell then, in a foetal crouch, his face touching the stony square. The man buckled the belt around his hard, narrow middle, and dragged the boy up by the slack of his shirt. He said something in *creole* and the boy, shivering, searched the pocket of his short trousers and handed Alex's quarter to the man. The elders sat straight in their cane chairs. There was no sound in the square.

As the punisher turned to face the elders, the sun struck a slate sheen off his brow, showed the knit black hair, the official cap pushed back at a careless angle.

Deliberately, like a fisherman casting, he tossed the quarter across the square in a high curve, dropping it exactly at the foot of the balcony steps. Then, his uniform and position still unidentified, he walked with long strides to the market, pushing past a cluster of watchers at the entrance. The boy ran for cover among the high old houses at the other side of the square. The elders leaned back in their chairs, drawing on their narrow cigarillos. Alex Cole looked at the coin below him, then went back into the store.

As he pushed open the screen door, Margaret backed away from it and sat down on the bench by the wall. She shook her head as though recovering from a dizzy spell. 'I feel sick. Sick to my stomach. It was just *disgusting*.'

She looked at him. 'You should have stopped it, Alex. You should have *done* something.'

He heard her start to cry. 'I felt,' he began. 'Margaret, I felt I had no right.'

'But that's nonsense, Alex. Nonsense.'

He waited, not looking at her, sure that her tears would not last. She had hoped so much for this trip; she had wanted so much that they would not be 'just tourists.' She had been sure of their ability to go off the beaten track, to see the country, to meet its people. It could not end like this. Not in a blunder, in a gaucheness, a 'disgusting' incident. He wondered how she would tell it, back home in Toronto. For she *would* tell it. Would it become a moral tale, a homily on the differences among peoples, or -God forbid – a humorous anecdote?

He heard her weeping cease. When he turned to her, she was rubbing her teary eyes with the back of her hand, as a cat does, washing. He handed her his handkerchief, saw her begin to smile.

'Well,' she said. 'We've found out one thing. They're certainly a horse of a different colour down here, aren't they?'

He took the roll of film containing the boy's pictures out of his pocket and left it on the counter of the store. He picked up the camera, hesitated, then strung it around his neck, in penance. He took his wife's arm, led her towards the door. 'Come on, dear,' he said. 'Time to go now.'

HEARTS AND FLOWERS

'Turkey and all the trimmings,' said the city editor, a knife-thin native of Saskatchewan whose public persona had been moulded by exposure to a movie version of *The Front Page*. 'It's part of a publicity gimmick in the fundraising campaign for the Old Bowerie Mission. On Christmas Eve the Mission will round up thirty, forty bums and give them a turkey dinner. There'll be carol singing, too. I've assigned you a photographer. It should make a nice little feature story for Christmas Day. Okay?'

The okay was rhetorical. He was the boss. As the photographer and I buckled on our overshoes, the city editor looked up from his desk and issued a last-minute directive.

'Hearts and flowers, kid. Remember to write it up hearts and flowers.'

Hearts and ... Snowbanks piled up along the main shopping streets of Montreal like mountains of dirty laundry, a glaze of ice on the tram tracks, a stalling and jangling of snow-laden trolley-car wires, a panic of shoppers pouring in and out of the stores – it took us an hour to cross the city.

At the Old Bowerie Mission, a long, grey barrack in a snowdrifted side street, all was efficiency and hearty welcome. We were expected.

'Howie Minchip's my name. I'm in charge here.' This, with a firm YMCA handshake and a no-cavity smile. Blue-blazered, grey-flannelled, his corn-silk hair shorn to a trim stubble, his skin pink from innumerable locker-room showers, he turned to his aides and spoke in capitals. 'The Press Has Arrived. Get The Men Into The Dining Hall. Mustn't Keep the Press Waiting.'

Merry Christmas – Joyeux Noel announced the impartial holly wreaths which lined the long corridor. 'Every decoration handmade personally by our residents,' Mr Minchip told us. No, there were not just residents at this Christmas dinner. 'Like in the Bible, we went out into the highways and the byways and picked our guests up. The last shall be first, eh? That's maybe an angle for your story.'

As for the residents, no one was permitted to spend more than three consecutive nights in the Mission. 'But we have regulars, of course.' The men checked into the Mission at six each evening, underwent a compulsory shower and a cursory medical inspection and then were issued nightshirts, a 'slice' and soup. Lights out at eight. In the morning, after a slice and coffee, they were on their way. 'Total charge, forty cents. Of course, we lose money on it.'

Which was why we were covering this Christmas

dinner, explained Mr Crump, of Canadian United Fundraisers, who waited for us at the entrance to the dining hall. 'With your newspaper story backed by pictures, the general public will see a visual and textual presentation of the Mission at work. And Christmas is the time for giving, right?'

The forty-odd men waiting in the dining hall had not yet taken their seats. Mr Minchip fixed that. 'All right now, fellas, let's get into two lines; come on, TWO LINES, form on the left, get your trays and pick up the food at the hatch.'

Unemployed miners and construction workers, lumberjacks laid off in mid-season, old winos and middle-aged beer hounds, a few lonely boys stranded in the big city, several immigrants who not found God's Own Country – they were a strangely pathetic group. They wore windbreakers, lumberjackets and army surplus overcoats. There wasn't much talk. They were solitaries. Few had buddies here. In two shuffling crocodile lies they circled the long trestle dining tables, picked up trays and cutlery and moved towards the serving hatches.

'Hold it!' Mr Minchip called. 'Hold it, fellas.' He turned to us. 'You want a picture of the chow line?'

The photographer, his Speed Graphic still hooded in its snowproof bag, shook his head. 'Look, it's a real turkey dinner,' Mr Minchip urged. 'All the trimmings – cranberry sauce, roast potato, bread stuffing. Plum pudding to follow. That's a dollar-fifty meal in any restaurant.'

But the photographer refused to bite. Solemn as children, the guests collected their food, moved to the tables and sat down. On each man's tray was a rolled-up paper party hat of the sort that come out of Christmas crackers. Mr Minchip excused himself and mounted a rostrum. Foursquare, he faced the room. 'Wait a minute, fellas. Wait until everybody is seated before we start, eh, fellas?'

Men who had picked up their forks put them down again. One or two whispered to their neighbours.

'Now, fellas, you see those party favours in front of you? They're hats. I want everybody to put a hat on, so's we can take a picture. Okay, fellas?'

Fingers, more used to laying bricks and lifting axes, carefully unpeeled the strips of paper. Some of the hats tore and fell apart. Mission aides ran up and down the lines of tables distributing spares. Finally, everyone had some coloured paper on his head. Or almost everyone. For it was then that I noticed Red.

He sat at the centre of a table near the wall, directly underneath coloured photographs of the Queen and Prince Philip. He was a large, middle-aged man with a ginger beard as thick as a broom. Rivers of tiny blue veins were mapped on the blotched skin of his drinker's face, and a red tartan lumberjack shirt was open at the neck to show the greyish beginnings of old-fashioned long under- wear. He seemed used and soiled by life. But he did not pick up his paper hat. Mr Minchip, anxious to give us our photograph, had overlooked him.

'All right now, fellas, hold it! We'll eat in a minute. But, first of all, I want you to take these leaflets we're passing out. We want to get a shot of everybody singing and having fun. We've got a Christmas carol printed on the leaflet and we're going to sing a couple of verses. Okay, fellas?'

At a signal from Mr Minchip, a blue-blazered aide sat down at an upright piano and struck a chord. Our photographer circled the tables looking for a likely pictorial composition.

'Okay now, fellas,' Mr Minchip said. 'God rest ye merry, gentlemen, let nothing you dismay. All together now, one, two, three—'

A churchly pause, a few congregational coughs and, following the lead given by Mr Michip's basso, voices rose in watery disharmony.

'God rest ye mer-ry, gen-tle-men . . .'

The photographer, suddenly deciding on the royal photographs as a suitable background, stopped, sighted his Speed Graphic and braced his legs for a shot. The men sat back, leaflets in hand, singing the verse. All except one. Red broke his roll in two, picked up his fork and began to eat. The photographer lowered his camera.

'Hold it!' Mr Minchip yelled. 'Hold it, fellas. Hey, *you*.'

Red continued to eat. His bearded jaws masticated turkey. His head was bent forward as though he ate alone in some lonely late-night diner.

'Hey there. Fella with the red beard. Come on now, fella.'

Still eating, Red turned his head, looked along the table and up at the rostrum, his blear eyes giving no sign that they had seen anything. Still eating, he lowered his head to his plate. Mr Minchip jumped off the rostrum, doubling quickly towards the trouble spot. 'Come on now, fella, put that fork down! Be a sport, fella, you're holding us up.'

Everyone waited. Above Red's head the Queen smiled bravely. Prince Philip looked stern, as though some errant industrialist had refused to pull his finger out. Red finished his mouthful and then, suddenly, stood up, rocking the table with his boozer's paunch. His huge hands closed into fists. Mr Minchip back-stepped.

'Hey,' Red said, staring drunkenly at the room. 'Man wants us to sing. Well, twenty, thirty fellas like us, we sing Christmas carols, we make a buck. We go out in the street, a couple of guys collect and the rest sing, we clear a stack of dimes, you bet your goddam life. We take the man's sheet of paper and go outside, we make money for wine and beer. Jugs of wine. Okay?'

'Now, wait a minute,' Mr Minchip said, but the rows of tables were a thick hum of excitement. A young lumber-jack jumped up, yelling: 'He's right, he's right!'

'Come on, then,' Red shouted. 'Leave the goddam Mission grub. We want wine. Come on, man wants us to sing, we'll sing.'

Of course, not everyone moved. Not even half of them. Old men and some immigrants who had not understood sat patiently waiting for the programme to continue. Deserted by his neighbours, a frightened boy pretended to study his leaflet. But fifteen or sixteen men, the jacks, the winos, the desperate, were on their feet, thumping through the dining hall, following Red's lurching, purposeful lead. Mr Minchip caught my arm. 'Don't worry, we'll regroup the seating arrangements—'

I did not wait. I ran down the corridor and out into the late afternoon snows. Some fifteen men stood on the pavement, half-uncertain, half-regretful. It was the moment when revolutions fail. But I heard Red shout: 'Beer, wine. Gallons of wine. Let's get it!'

He lurched among them, lining them up, their leaflets in their hands. Himself roaring out the words, he led them into the Main.

'God rest ye mer-ry, gen-tle-men, let nothing you dismay—'

They forged up towards the shopping centres, ignoring the sidewalk, stopping traffic as they marched on in a ragged, disorderly, singing phalanx. At the second verse all trace of embarrassment left their voices and the words were roared out in defiance. Like outriders on the edge of a column, three of the old winos doffed their caps, running in and out among the burghers, collecting and entreating. I saw dimes, quarters, even dollar bills going into those caps as the column trudged towards the rich pickings of St Catherine Street, singing over and over those verses Mr Minchip had provided. Bemused shoppers clogged the sidewalks to watch. There would be wine tonight in all the taverns of the Main. At the head of his band of incredible carollers, Red sang loud and clear:

> God rest ye merry, gentlemen,
> Let nothing you dismay.

It was hearts and flowers, all right. Hearts and flowers.

PRELIMINARY PAGES FOR A WORK OF REVENGE

The characters in this work are meant to be real.
References to persons living and dead are intended.

Are there fifteen people in the world who will be afraid when they read this paragraph? No. That, in itself, is a comment on my insignificance. Are there fifteen people who will become uneasy on reading it? I think so. Almost half my life is over and I have known many people. I know things about some of them which they would not like to see written down. Are you uneasy, S—? Or you, F—? Or you, my once dear T—? Why do I not spell out your names? Well, for one thing I have known more than one S— in my life. If I can make two of you uneasy, then so much the better. For another, were I to reveal your disparate identities you would possibly band together in order to silence me. In these preliminary pages I wish to engage you singly, yet collectively, to reveal my identity to each of you in turn, yet to preserve a final anonymity so that none of you will be sure you are thinking about the same person. That is my strategy.

My second preliminary page is reserved for a quotation. Authors usually add a quotation as a propitiatory rite in hopes that the wise saying of some great man will induce in the reader a similar respect for the idiocies contained in the work which will follow it. My intention is not propitiatory. It is minatory. Here is my quotation.

'Life being what it is, one dreams of revenge.'
Paul Gauguin

You know what I mean, don't you? Very well then, let us turn the page.

ACKNOWLEDGEMENTS

The author does not wish to express his gratitude to anyone. He has no reasons to be grateful. He does, however, wish to acknowledge that parts of this work have been provided him unwittingly by relatives and friends, enemies and acquaintances. The uses he intends to make of the facts, lies, rumours, scandals and secrets so provided shall be his own. He will attempt to make his own truth for, like Pilate, he knows only that truth is not the accurate rendition of facts. Was the man they crucified that Friday afternoon an obscure agitator who had made a small stir in Jerusalem? Or was he the son of God? We still have no facts. We have religions.

Turn the page.

Some of you may have turned first to this page. Go back. I shall not reveal myself so easily. The name I have used on the first page of this work is mine, yet not mine. It is my *nom de plume*. If you do not believe that it is the name of a professional writer you have merely to look up certain volumes of bibliography published in the United States and Great Britain during the past five years. I say this to warn you that these pages are written in the expectation of seeing them published. I am not writing from an asylum. I know you and you know me. These pages reached you postmarked with the name of the city in which you were born. But I do not live there now. I merely had the letters sent from there as, shall we say, an *aide-mémoire* to some of you. The postmark ensured that you would open the letter, for no other postmark can compete in authority with the place of one's birth. It is what we fled: it may, at any time, reach up to reclaim us.

So, there is no error. Your name and address have been carefully checked and unless you are at the moment reading someone else's mail, you are one of the persons with whom I am concerned. Or let me say that you may be one of the persons concerned: the decision is yours: However, I anticipate myself. So – about the author:

I am that person you insulted. I am that person you forgot. I am the one you do not speak of, the person you hope never to meet again. I am the one you said something mean and spiteful about and I have heard what you said. I am that friend who fell out of fashion, whose reminiscences about old times you found boring, whose dinner invitation you did not return, whose address you did not keep. I am that person you never phoned back. I am that person you flattered then ignored, the one who rang your doorbell many times while you sat like a statue inside, hoping I would go away. I am the one whose footsteps you heard going down the stairs, who knew you were there and hated you for it. For you did not deceive me. Did you honestly think that people like me are ever deceived by evasion and excuses? Unlike the successful friends you now court, we are not busy; we plan each visit and depend on it. Perhaps you *did* forget our appointment. Perhaps you *were* out. But then, if you really forgot, is that not a far greater wrong?

I am that person you betrayed. I am the one who confided my faults, my shames, my fears. I am the one to whom you swore secrecy, whose confidences you promised to respect. But one night at a party when someone wondered out loud, when someone told a garbled version of the facts I had confided to you and someone else contradicted them, you who knew the truth, could not keep your mouth shut. You shook your head wisely at the talkers, took a deep breath and, for the moment's pleasure of having an audience, you told my secrets out. And then, having betrayed me once, you continued to do it. Two years later, all my shames and fears had been fitted into a repertoire of amusing stories to delight your new marriage partner. (Who does not know me: whom you did not even know

when I told you those private things.) You know what I am
talking about, don't you?

I am the person who loved you. You said you loved me
but behind my back you told others that you were merely
'fond' of me. Yet I am the one in whose arms you wept, the
one who sat up all night with you, the one who helped you
when things went wrong. It was comforting to have me
on display at that time for I so obviously loved you. I was
the two ears, the tail and all four hoofs to hold aloft in the
plaza while you waited for someone better. I am the one
who walked away and did not look back, the one who hung
up the receiver, the familiar voice which was never the
same again. I can tell you now that I cried. I cried because
you told me not to worry, that nothing was changed. I
cried because I guessed then that you had already made
your secret plans to leave me. I was right, wasn't I? Later,
you remember, when it was all over and we knew it, you
said you were trying to be honest. You said we were never
suited to each other. You knew I would understand, you
said. Did I understand? Do I? What would you think of
me, if you were me? I know that you have been in and out
of the place where I live many times. I know that you have
never phoned me. I know that you never will phone me.

Some of you, reading this, may decide it is not
addressed to you. You do not know me from these pages.
That is true. To some of you, I was a child. To you, my
classmates, I address the following.

As a child I did not believe that I was clever. I feared
myself to be stupid and cowardly and believed that I would
be a disappointment to all who knew me. I read a great

deal and like many unsure children I had a taste for tragic endings. But in my reading I discovered that, to fall from the heights of tragedy, heroes must first scale the peaks of achievement. In books, I searched for a suitable daydream. When I was fourteen we were asked to write an essay about our ambitions in life. I wrote all night. I was, for the first time in my life, inspired. (The first and last time if you except this work.) I wrote that I would become a great poet, that I would devote my life to the composition of a masterpiece and that, at the age of thirty, coughing blood in a last consumptive frenzy, I hoped to die, my gift still clean and unmuddled. This essay I submitted to my English master who, the following day, came to my desk, took my ear between his nicotined thumb and forefinger and led me before the class to read my essay aloud. Oh, what a fine foil I must have seemed for the exercise of his lumpish pedagogic wit, what a perfect victim with which to win amusement from a class of captive boys!

But he is dead now, my master. I can no longer hate him for his use of me as hunchback for his sallies. Nor can I hate my classmates for the larger diversion you staged after school. Why should I? At the time, the incident seemed the greatest triumph of my life.

You may remember how a much larger audience assembled as I was dragged to the school drinking fountain, ducked under it and held until water ran down my spine, dripped into my trousers, trickled down my skinny legs to fill my socks and shoes. You may remember that, after my ducking, I was forced to read my essay once more. Your motives were just, I suppose. You wanted to knock the pretensions from under me, to teach me the lesson I have been too long in learning. But I learned nothing. Soaking wet, my clothes torn, I read my essay, but with pride now, screaming out that I would do everything I had promised in it. And all of you, watching my pale face and trembling shoulders, hearing the true fanatic in my thin defiant scream, all of you turned away, uneasy of me. Because conviction - even a wrong conviction – makes the rest of us uneasy. For the first time in my life I had won. My own unsurety died and for the remainder of my years at school I grew in the wind of your disapproval. Your doubts that day made me victim – the victim I still remain – of my own uncertain boast.

For I did not become great. I had no vocation for greatness. At thirty, instead of coughing blood, I bled rectally from haemorrhoids. I who boasted to you that I would never settle for the ordinary avocations you proposed have settled instead for failure. Yet in writing this I show that I have not even the dignity of a man who has accepted a fate, no matter how despicable. I am still unable to agree to my failure because on that day, when by your fear of me you gave me a taste of what greatness might bring me, my course was set, suddenly, haphazardly, yet with no possible alternative routing, towards a destiny I was not fit to accomplish. Oh, how I wish you had succeeded in drenching all my foolish hopes under that fountain. For who is more unworthy than a fool who boasts of talents he does not possess? Who more contemptible than the false artist posturing through life as he spews out his tiny frauds? What spectacle more truly degrading than a would-be

Rimbaud, covered in the vomit of sickly pastiche, crying out his genius and his purity from a mouth filled with rotten teeth? I am that man. Are you responsible for the monstrous imposter I have become? Not you alone. There are others.

I reveal myself to those others now. You are my peers. You are those who encouraged me, those who, sinning against uncomfortable truths, were always willing and eager to admit a new accomplice to the small smelly circles of your self-love and self-deceit. You are the members of cliques and coteries – do not deny it for, of course, everyone will deny that he is the member of a clique – but let me describe you to yourselves and ask if you can wear the shoe. You are the small uncertain talents of our time, ever ready to arrange a panel, lunch a critic, flatter a would-be disciple, praise an enemy if he has the power to hurt you, betray a friend whose reputation you hear is on the fade. You are the readers of reviews, not of books, the hiders in your attics of pictures now said to have gone out of style. Must I go on? You know what I am talking about, don't you? I am one of you or was one of you until I lost my grip on the tiny fringe of the curtain we mutually clutched to hide our falsities from the light of truth.

Truth. I cry out the word with fetid breath. Truth was to have been my redemption from the things that you and you and I and I have made of me. I am my own Judas. In writing these pages I have once again demonstrated that I am not worthy to attempt the truth. I make you the confession now, that as I started to write I was at once deflected from the truth. Truth could wait, in the moment of writing, I knew it was money I sought. I excused myself by thinking that I cannot write my work of truth until I have enough money to complete it. And so, I knew that if I could strike at the guilt in half your hearts, some of you might send me small sums of money which would help me continue in this work. I excused myself by swearing (falsely) that despite these sums of money I would not allow myself to be deflected from writing the truth about you: a blackmailer is under no obligation to keep his word. And so, by this muddled morality – despicable, of course, but an important part of the truth about me – I hoped to gain time to write a work so terrible in its truth that it would revenge me forever. But what is the truth I seek? On whom must I revenge myself?

On you who has falsely flattered me? On you who did not love me enough? On you who scorned me? Can I hold you responsible for the man I was, the man I am, the man I will be? Which of us can tell who is at fault? I can only say that long ago your unwillingness to let me dream prevented for years my true awakening. I wonder now what you would say if you could see me now. For what is the purpose of these preliminary pages. Before I begin to write this work I want to know that I am not, once again, mistaken in my purpose. I want to know if you have rec-ognised me, if you remember me. Can you see me? Can you see the man who sits at a desk, trying with a pen – that ludicrous weapon which conceit once forced into his hand – to reach you across the waste of twenty years? Look, look and you will see me. Here I am. I am here. Can you see me now? Do you laugh? Or do you weep?